Good character, like good soup, is most often homemade.

—An Amish Proverb

Sugarcreek Amish Mysteries

Blessings in Disguise
Where Hope Dwells
The Buggy before the Horse
A Season of Secrets
O Little Town of Sugarcreek
Off the Beaten Path
Peace Like a River
Simply Vanished
A Stitch in Time
Mason Jar Mayhem
When There's a Will
Shoo, Fly, Shoo!

Shoo, FLY, Shoo!

AMY LILLARD

Guideposts

New York

Sugarcreek Amish Mysteries is a trademark of Guideposts.

Published by Guideposts Books & Inspirational Media
110 William Street
New York, NY 10038
Guideposts.org

Cover and interior design by Müllerhaus
Cover illustration by Bill Bruning, represented by Deborah Wolfe, LTD.
Typeset by Aptara, Inc.

Printed and bound in the United States of America
10 9 8 7 6 5 4 3

To Martha, Anna Mae, and Girlie for teaching me
all about Amish dairy farms.
This book would not have been the same
without your help!

CHAPTER ONE

Sirens blaring, lights twirling, Sugarcreek's finest raced past the Miller farm.

"That looks like trouble." Cheryl Cooper turned to her friend as the sirens wailed by.

"Oh, this can't be good." A frown creased Naomi Miller's brow. "The Albert Yoders live down there."

Cheryl had heard of the family. Albert Yoder was a successful dairy farmer, producing what some considered the finest milk in the community. "You think there's trouble at the Yoder farm?"

Naomi continued to stare off into the distance, her gaze fixed in the direction where the police cars disappeared. "Rebekah Yoder is going to have a baby. This time has not been easy for her."

Cheryl followed Naomi's gaze but shook her head. "Why would Rebekah need a police car if she's gone into labor?"

"I do not know."

But Cheryl did. This was trouble of a different sort.

"I need to go down there." Naomi whirled on her heel and headed back into the house.

Cheryl had come out to the Miller farm for a quick afternoon visit and to see a new animal for their petting zoo, a black alpaca with long eyelashes and a sweet face. Naomi had been asking her for days to come out and see the creature, but Cheryl had to put her off. Summertime in Sugarcreek meant more tourists than locals, and the Swiss Miss had been busier than ever.

"You mean now?" she asked as Naomi rushed from the house and whistled for her horse. "It would be so much quicker in my car."

Naomi gave her buggy horse a pat on the neck and then turned back to Cheryl. "Thank you, Cheryl Cooper."

The pair hopped into the car, and Cheryl headed in the direction where the police cars had disappeared. She couldn't imagine what police cars had to do with a pregnant woman, and she wasn't sure she wanted to know. She cast a quick look at Naomi. Her friend sat ramrod straight in the passenger side, hands folded primly in her lap, eyes trained firmly ahead. She wasn't sure either one of them was prepared for what could be waiting at the Yoder farm. She could only pray that it was nothing as grisly as prime-time television portrayed.

A few minutes later Cheryl pulled her little blue sedan into utter chaos. She cut the engine as Naomi got out of the car and rushed into the fray, undoubtedly looking for Rebekah Yoder.

Cheryl paused for a moment just to take it all in. Aside from the two police cars, there was a fire truck, a bulldozer, and a backhoe. The police officers were talking to different people. Chief Twitchell was taking notes on his little memo book as an older Amish man spoke. His beard was completely gray, though his eyes flashed blue fire behind his wire-rimmed glasses. He gestured wildly with his hands as Twitchell nodded and continued to write.

Cheryl watched, entranced. She had never seen anyone Amish be that animated before. He was all but shouting as he gestured and pointed. Whatever had happened, it seemed like a pretty big deal. But if the police were talking to the farm owner, Cheryl could only assume that the older man was none other than Albert Yoder. If that was the case, then hopefully everything was okay with Rebekah.

She allowed her gaze to run over the crowd of people. Aside from the chief, there were two policemen, four or five men in hard hats, a handful of firemen, a bevy of children, and at least a dozen gawkers. No doubt police sirens brought out the Amish and English alike.

She spotted Naomi in the bustle of people. Her friend wound through the crowd until she reached an Amish woman about the same age as she, though of opposite build. The woman wore a green dress, a black day apron, and seemed as round as Naomi was thin. As Cheryl watched, Naomi clasped the woman's hands into her own and pressed them to her heart.

As reserved as Naomi was, this just proved how concerned she had been. Cheryl breathed a small sigh of relief. At least there wasn't anything wrong with Rebekah or her baby, though the farm she wasn't so sure about.

The Yoders' barn looked as if it had been chopped in half. The side that was still standing leaned a bit to the side. Cheryl grew nervous just looking at it. Someone, most likely the construction crew, had braced it up with poles and rope, but Cheryl wasn't certain those measures would be enough to keep it upright if a strong wind blew through. The other side had been leveled, the debris tossed into a Big Green Container. The field where it stood was a complete mess. Mud caked everything around it from the men's boots to the caterpillar tracks on the big yellow equipment. A spout of water bubbled up like a mountain spring. A couple of the hard-hat men worked to stop the gurgle, completely ignoring the fray around them.

She sidled up to the nearest person. "What happened here?"

The Amish man grinned, though the action didn't reach his hard green eyes. "Someone's stealing old Yoder's milk."

His milk? Cheryl allowed her gaze to wander around the farm once more. "And that's why they have the bulldozers out here?"

The man shook his head. He looked to be about the same age as "old Yoder," and she noticed that his straw hat had a hole in one side. He wore the standard blue shirt and black pants, and like most of the Plain men standing around, his boots had seen more than their fair share of dirt. "Some of that is on account of the manure. *Ja*, Albert has a mess on his hands." He gave a small chuckle.

"Manure?" She turned to him, but he had already walked away. As she watched, he crossed the road and to the farm on the other side. It looked about the same as the Yoder place—big rambling white house with a barn and a silo off to one side. Though this man's barn was complete, and there were no bubbling streams chugging up from busted water pipes.

Cheryl watched him go. For the most part the residents of Sugarcreek, both Amish and English, were the nicest people she'd ever want to meet. But there were some...

This man—Chupp if the name on the mailbox was correct, and she had no reason to believe otherwise—seemed to take great pleasure in the fact that his neighbor was having problems.

With a shake of her head, she looked back at the clusters of people and vehicles but couldn't see Naomi or Rebekah Yoder any longer.

Chupp's words had piqued her interest. How exactly did one steal milk? Only one way to find that out, she thought, and eased her way closer to Chief Twitchell.

"If the milk has been disappearing for months, why haven't you called me before?" the chief asked. Cheryl resisted the urge to lean in closer so she could hear them better, but Albert Yoder was angry enough that his voice was far from soft.

"You know how young people are these days." Albert shook his head. "I just figured they did not get all the cows in the barn. Or maybe they just missed the milking altogether. But I was with them last night, every step of the way. Then come this morning the tank was only half full—and after I did the morning milking too."

The chief made a couple more notes on his little pad. Then trained his gaze on Albert. Cheryl stayed well enough behind him so she was out of Twitchell's line of sight. He would surely tell her to move along if he knew she was listening in. But there was something odd about the situation. Or maybe it was all the other chaos at the farm. The half-torn-down barn and the earth-moving equipment. Even the muddy field. It had recently rained, leaving soggy earth in its wake. And the temperatures had turned cooler, even though today was the first day of July, leaving the moisture in place for a lot longer than normal. But that still didn't account for the growing pond off to one side of the barn.

"What about a leak?" the chief asked. He pointed to the water-logged ground.

"There is no leak in the milk vat," Albert said emphatically. "The water came from a busted pipe. These guys hit a water pipe trying to level the farm. Folks just do not do a job like they used to." He shook his head.

"And you think that excuses the illegal sellin' of raw milk?"

"I did not do anything wrong."

"That's not mine to decide, Albert."

"I thought a man had a right to defend himself in this country," Albert said. "You come out here saying I have been selling milk, and I tell you someone has been stealing it."

The chief stiffened, and Cheryl had a feeling he was resisting the urge to pinch the bridge of his nose. She couldn't say as she blamed him. Sometimes talking with the Amish was like speaking English in a foreign land. The less dealings an Amish person had with the English, the harder it was for them to communicate with each other.

Whatever had happened, Albert Yoder clearly didn't understand.

The chief pulled a pair of handcuffs from the back of his belt and held them in front of him. "Now, Albert, I don't want any trouble."

Albert Yoder's eyes grew wide as he stared at the metal bracelets.

"I don't want any trouble," the chief repeated. "But I gotta take you in. I've got witnesses and a warrant."

"But…," Albert started, but his words stopped dead as the handcuffs clicked into place on his wrist. To the chief's credit, he didn't handcuff Albert with his hands behind him. Instead he allowed them to remain in front.

Off to the side, even amid the fray of noise and activity, Cheryl heard someone draw a sharp breath. She turned as Rebekah Yoder came waddling toward her husband.

"Be strong, Wife," Albert said with a quick nod. Unlike English couples who would embrace and perhaps kiss before one was led away, they just stared at each other, somehow relaying information that only the two of them knew with just their gaze. It was special and unnerving all at the same time. Then the connection was broken as the chief steered Albert Yoder toward the back door of his car.

Cheryl felt rather than saw Naomi come up beside her. And together they watched as the chief came around to his side of the car, started the engine, and backed out of the drive. One by one, spectators dispersed. The police left, the firemen left, and the construction workers went back to work. What had been a near circus of activity slowed until only a few of them remained: Naomi, Cheryl, Rebekah Yoder, and the passel of kids that belonged to her and Albert. Everyone just stood and watched as if somehow the chief was going to bring Albert back and say that it was all just a bad joke.

"I'm so confused," Cheryl said. She let her gaze drift between Naomi and Rebekah. Surely whatever happened must have been very serious for the chief to take Albert away so close to the time for his child to be born. True, the Amish weren't quite as narcissistic when it came to childbirth and their children, but they were human beings. It was obvious that Albert cared for his wife very much. And though Cheryl herself had never experienced it, she knew that labor had to be a traumatic experience. She could only hope that Albert would be out of jail in time to see his baby come into the world.

Naomi pressed her lips together. "The chief seems to believe that Albert Yoder has been out selling raw milk."

"I do not understand why he would think that," Rebekah added. "We have plenty of buyers for the milk. We always sell it to well-known companies. Why would they think he would start selling it on the black market?"

Cheryl bit back a smile at the words. It wasn't appropriate to laugh at a time like this, but to hear "black market" come from the lips of an Amish woman was almost more than she could take. Rebekah had a point though. If they had buyers for their milk on a continual basis, why should he sell the raw milk now?

"The chief mentioned it's illegal to sell raw milk?" Cheryl asked. She never really thought about it much, but she supposed that raw milk had its host of issues. Listeria being among them. But she also knew that raw milk was in great demand with so many people going "organic" and eating "clean." No availability and great demand had created a black market for unprocessed milk. And as silly as it sounded, she had heard tales in New York of the police chasing down Amish dairy farmers who were selling their milk under the table, so to speak. One thing was certain: Listeria could be dangerous.

"I take it that Chief Twitchell didn't believe your arguments," Cheryl said, though she knew it had to be more than that.

"He said they had witnesses. But he would not tell me who they are," Rebekah said.

Of course not—the chief was anything but a fool. And the identity of witnesses of any sort was something that needed to be protected.

"Come." Naomi wrapped an arm around Rebekah's shoulders and led her toward the house. Without much else to do, Cheryl followed behind, as did six little girls. The oldest was around twelve, and their ages stair-stepped to the youngest who couldn't have been much more than three. She was a cute little cherub of a girl with Rebekah's dark hair and Albert's blue eyes. She had one arm wrapped around a doll and bent at the elbow with her thumb planted firmly in her mouth.

"I do not have any pie to offer you," Rebekah said apologetically.

"We did not come for pie," Naomi said. "We came because we were concerned about you."

The women settled around the kitchen table while the girls filed off into another room. Rebekah rubbed a hand across her swollen belly. "We are okay." *For now* hung in the air between them. "How long can they keep Albert in jail?" She directed this at Cheryl.

"Oh my goodness," Naomi said. "I forgot to introduce you."

Rebekah shook her head. "We have not been introduced, but I have seen you around town. Cheryl Cooper. You are kin to Mitzi who owns the Swiss Miss."

"She's my aunt."

"What do you think? Will they keep my Albert for long?"

"I don't know," Cheryl said honestly. "Did the chief say if anyone was hurt?"

"He claims some people are sick because of Albert's milk," Rebekah said. "But he did not say if anyone was hurt badly or anything. I still do not see why they took him. Albert did not do this."

"Well, it's like . . ." Cheryl stopped, trying to form the words but falling short, way short of an explanation she thought Rebekah could understand. "They have to have some evidence in order to arrest Albert to start with." It wasn't what she wanted to say, but it was true all the same. "And then there are witnesses. Or so he says," Cheryl added. "But as far as how long they can keep him . . . They can hold him for forty-eight hours without formally charging him and then charge him after that. Then he would be allowed to have a bail hearing. As long as they agree to set bail. Then after that you would have the opportunity to bail him out of jail. But if you don't have the money to do that, then he would remain in jail until his court date."

Naomi and Rebekah wore matching frowns of confusion. Cheryl had tried to explain it as simply as she could, but for most Amish the US court system was an unexplainable labyrinth of mystery.

"I do not understand," Naomi said.

"*Maam.*" The three women turned as one of the Yoder daughters eased into the kitchen. "We milked the cows last night.

We did. *Daed* was even with us. And we have milked them every time before. I do not understand..." Tears welled in her blue eyes.

Her mother reached out a hand toward her. The young girl allowed herself to be cradled against Rebekah as she cried out her confusion. "They will not hurt Daed, will they?"

"No, Daughter, of course not." But from the look on her face, Cheryl knew that Rebekah Yoder was worried about the exact same thing.

Cheryl wished she had the words to better explain the situation to them. To help Rebekah and the rest of the family understand that Albert would be fine in jail. It wouldn't be comfortable. It wouldn't be the place he wanted to be, but Chief Twitchell was a fair man, and he would keep Albert separated from the English prisoners if only just to shelter his beliefs.

"What are we going to do?" the young girl asked.

Rebekah smoothed the sides of her daughter's hair, her lack of a prayer *kapp* testimony to the fact that she was under thirteen. "We are making a plan now, Abigail. You go on and tell your sisters that everything will be all right." Her mouth trembled as she said the words, but she stiffened her shoulders as if that alone would give them all the courage they needed to get through this.

"Yes, Maam."

"Go on now." Rebekah urged her to leave the room.

Abigail did so, though reluctantly, and Rebekah turned back to the two of them. The look in her eyes was so beseeching, so heartbroken and concerned that Cheryl almost wept. It was one thing to understand the basics of how the courts worked and the charges brought against a person, and quite another to be totally lost in what was basically a foreign land.

"What do we do?" Rebekah asked.

Cheryl wished she knew. "What all did the chief say while he was here?"

Rebekah folded her hands across her big belly. "I did not hear all of it. I just know that Albert had gone out to burn the trash and do a couple more chores. Then the next thing I know I hear police sirens. It took me a while to get out there. I do not move as quickly these days." She shot them both a rueful smile. "The chief said something about the milk, and Albert started arguing with him. But there has been milk gone."

"And you think someone stole it?" Cheryl asked.

How did one steal milk? The stainless-steel container they held it in was huge, and the milk was pumped out by truck. It wasn't like someone could just come up and pour themselves a container and walk away. Could they?

"Yes. Yes, I do."

Cheryl could mull over the situation as long as she wanted to, but it would do no good until she knew all the details. "Rebekah, why don't you start at the beginning?"

Rebekah took a deep breath then ran a reassuring hand over the mound of her stomach. "I guess it started about two months ago. I was standing here in the kitchen when Albert came in. I could hear the milk truck outside running. Albert said that the holding tank didn't have enough milk in it."

"So it had some milk in it?" Cheryl asked.

"Yes. But not all of it. See, we milk on average four times before the milk truck comes in. That builds us so many gallons, which fills the container nearly to the top, but when they started pumping the milk out..."

"Some of it was gone," Cheryl finished for her.

"*Most* of it was gone," Rebekah corrected.

"Then what happened?" Cheryl asked.

"As you can imagine, Albert was not very happy about that. He called the girls in and talked to them." She shook her head. "Quite sternly, as a matter of fact. He told them about their responsibilities and what they owe to the family, the usual. I mean, sometimes if he is not out there with them, the chores do not get done as properly as he might have liked. But they are all good girls. I cannot imagine that they would completely *not* milk the cows. In fact, I think Albert would have known that the next morning when he went out to do the milking."

"How's that?" Cheryl asked. What she knew about milking cows could fit on a sticky note with room to write the Lord's Prayer a couple of times and not even touch the back.

"The cows would have been very uncomfortable."

Because they would have been full of milk. Cheryl nodded, silently vowing to find out just a little bit more about how dairy farms worked. She would need to if she was going to help the Yoders.

"So they promised to do better when they were milking, and it seemed for a while that they did. Then a week or so later the same thing happened. The girls promised that they had done what they were supposed to do. I really think Albert wanted to believe them. He called a man out to inspect the tank and make sure that it didn't have any leaks. Of course with all the work that we're having done now"—she waved an expressive hand in the direction of the barn—"it was hard to tell if there was any milk spilled or not. The ground has been wet; the barn is half torn down. There was just no way to know for sure."

"Except to have it inspected?" Cheryl asked.

"Ja."

"Then what happened?" Cheryl asked.

Rebekah's brow wrinkled with thought. "I guess it was about that time that the horses got loose."

Cheryl shook her head. "In the road?"

Rebekah nodded. "We got up one morning and all the horses were just running around. We had to chase them all down and put them back in the corral. It took us two days to find the gelding Albert bought for my buggy. I guess they called him Lightning Bug for a reason. He was the racehorse, you know. Retired now, but he still likes to run. I was not sure we would ever catch him."

Cheryl wasn't sure what runaway horses had to do with stolen milk, but she didn't want to interrupt Rebekah. The two things could have a bearing on each other, or one or both of them could just be a high school prank.

School had been out for a month now, and most kids were starting to get restless. Well, the English kids were, though she wouldn't place all of it at their feet. Some of the more adventuresome Amish kids on *rumspringa* could get a little rowdy as well. As a town they didn't have a lot of problems with it, but it still could rear its ugly head from time to time.

"So the milk was missing, and the horses ran away. Anything else?"

"There have been a lot of little things." Rebekah pressed her lips together as if trying to remember, or maybe she was just trying to filter through what was important and what was not.

"What kind of little things?"

"Just little things," she said. "Sometimes we would come in and the horses would not have any water. We came back from church once and found all the hay had been busted up and knocked down from the hayloft. And I think someone might have poured salt on my tomato plants."

Any of those things could be high school pranks. And they sounded more like juvenile mischief than anything else. "What about the milk?" Naomi asked.

"The milk has been an ongoing problem."

Cheryl frowned. "Pardon my ignorance on the subject, but it can't just evaporate, can it?"

Naomi and Rebekah shared a small chuckle. "No," Rebekah said. "It cannot just evaporate."

"So that means one thing," Cheryl said.

Rebekah nodded. "It must be that someone is stealing our milk."

CHAPTER TWO

J ust before opening the next day, Naomi knocked on the door of the Swiss Miss then quietly let herself in.

Cheryl looked up from the inventory ledger she was updating and smiled at her friend. Sure, she left the door open for just these occasions, but some people were more joyous to receive than others.

"I hope you have some peach jam in there," Cheryl said with a nod toward the blue-painted wagon Naomi pulled behind her. "I'm almost out."

Naomi nodded, sending the untied strings of her prayer kapp dancing around her shoulders. "I do, ja."

Cheryl closed the ledger and went around to the front side of the counter to help Naomi unload the wagon. "Where's Levi this morning?" She couldn't help herself from asking, seeing that these days every time she opened her mouth Levi's name seemed to fly from her lips. It was a perplexing situation at best. And one that she wasn't sure had any sort of resolution. Best forget it right now and get over whatever obsession it was that she had with Levi Miller.

"He is with the alpaca," Naomi said. "The poor creature had a bad night. Cried and howled from dusk till dawn." Naomi shook her head. "It was worse than having a new puppy around."

With all the excitement of the day before, Cheryl had forgotten all about the new alpaca at the Millers' petting zoo. Funny how having your best friend's neighbor arrested could do that to a person. "Have you seen Rebekah?"

Naomi stopped pulling jars out of her wagon and gave a sigh. "I sent Caleb and Eli down to help this morning. But it is almost more than they can do without Albert around. Rebekah just cannot get out there and oversee the girls. Our family would like to help even more, but the petting zoo is so busy these days…" She pressed her lips together and shook her head.

"I take it she hasn't had the baby yet." Cheryl had been a little concerned that Rebekah might go into labor that night.

"*Ne.*" Naomi resumed her efforts to unload the wagon, though Cheryl could tell that her friend was worried. She also knew that when the time was right, Naomi would tell her what was on her mind. She just had to wait until then.

"Do you think someone is trying to sabotage the Yoders?"

That didn't take long. "I wouldn't know."

"But what do you think?" Naomi pressed.

"It could go either way, really. The question is why would somebody target the Yoders?"

Naomi lost a lot of starch at Cheryl's rebuttal. "I do not know, maybe all the mess with the manure?"

They finished unloading the wagon, and Cheryl stacked everything up on the counter so she could inventory it quickly. "I'm still not sure I understand the manure situation."

Naomi screwed up her face a little as if she were in deep thought. "It is hard to explain. But when the cows come into the barn they...you know...on their way there."

Cheryl managed to keep her lips straight even as they twitched, fighting to spread into a smile. "Okay."

"If the manure is on the ground out in the pasture and it starts to rain, then the manure just goes back into the earth."

"Makes sense."

"And when they are in the milking stalls, there is a special pit underneath for the manure."

Cheryl gave a quick nod. She remembered seeing something in an article about manure pits in the *Budget*. It was a story about a young boy who accidentally drove his skid loader into a manure pit. He had almost died but managed to get out without harm. The machinery, on the other hand, was not so lucky.

"Well, the Yoders' farm sits up just enough off the road and at a slant that when his cows are coming into the barn and they drop their manure and it happens to rain soon after, then the manure and dirt tends to run down into the road." Cheryl wasn't sure how many cows it would take to produce a mess big enough for someone to even care, but she supposed that if even ten cows did something like that twice a day, then the mess would be substantial.

"So why did they tear down his barn?"

Naomi leaned a little closer as if there were somebody around to overhear them. "They were not supposed to. I asked Rebekah yesterday, before they took Albert away. She said the men backed into that side of the barn, and it was like a domino effect." She used her hands to express one thing falling after another, complete with sound effects.

Again she had Cheryl fighting back a smile. "What do they do now?"

"Rebekah said they have to rebuild the barn and add a top covering for the path the cows use to come in. Because it is paved, it causes the problem with the manure. But once it is covered, then the workers can come through and shovel the manure off the path and back into the pit. Then when it rains, it will not run down into the road."

"Can they still milk the cows?"

"Of course. Thankfully the part where the actual milking takes place was unharmed. I would hate to think what would happen if they weren't able to milk for all this time."

It sounded mighty complicated to Cheryl, but she nodded politely anyway. "Did Rebekah tell you why they had all the earth-moving equipment?"

"Oh ja. They are trying to level out the farm so the land doesn't run into the road. It's not just manure, you know. Some of it is just plain mud."

"I guess that makes sense." Cheryl couldn't quite wrap her mind around it, but she would mull it over later and see if she could come to terms. But that wasn't the most important thing in yesterday's activities. "So if you sent Caleb and Eli out to help the Yoders, did they say Rebekah was doing okay?"

Naomi gave a small nod. "She is a strong woman. And she will manage. I just worry about the baby."

"I think we're all worried about the baby."

"Would you...?" Naomi shook her head. Then she took a deep breath as if gathering her courage. "Will you help Rebekah get Albert out of jail?"

As badly as Cheryl wanted to tell Naomi that she needed to not get involved with the situation with the Yoders, the image of Rebekah Yoder sitting at her kitchen table, a confused frown on her brow and slim hand pressed against her round belly, flashed through Cheryl's mind. For all their dealings with the English folks, some Amish people just seemed to be more sheltered than others. Cheryl had no idea how many English people the Yoders encountered on a daily or weekly basis, but she had a feeling that the man who drove the milk truck was about the only one most of them ever saw.

"I'll help," Cheryl heard herself say. "First thing we need to do is find out when they post bail for Albert Yoder."

Naomi pressed her lips together. "It is that Marvin Chupp," she said in what had to be the meanest comment Cheryl had ever heard her make.

"I beg your pardon?"

Naomi shook her head, once again sending her prayer kapp strings jiggling about. "Marvin Chupp. You were talking to him yesterday. He lives across the road from the Yoders." She looked around as if someone were about to overhear them. Cheryl still had a few minutes before she had to open the store, but Naomi wasn't the only Sugarcreek resident who would come in before hours. "I cannot help but believe he had something to do with it."

Cheryl thought back to her conversation with the Amish man the day before. He had seemed a little bit jovial about the trouble his neighbor was facing. "Do you think he was the one who complained about the manure?"

"Maybe. But it all started so long ago, I do not even remember when," Naomi said.

"What started?"

"Now I do not mean to be telling tales," Naomi began, "but the two of them have been at odds for years and years. Some folks just aren't meant to get along, I guess."

"I take it the two of them are less than friends."

"Albert is about as nice a man as you would ever want to meet. And most folks around here think his milk is the best. That is the rumor anyhow. And it seems like no matter how much Marvin tries to get ahead of Albert, he just cannot do it."

"What do you mean?" Cheryl frowned.

"Once, Marvin started feeding his cows some sort of new alfalfa hay, and the next thing I know Albert has gone completely organic. That is a big deal these days, ja?"

Cheryl nodded. "It is."

"Albert buys four new cows, Marvin buys five. I do not know what started it or how it came to be. But there is a competition between those two men."

"A competition great enough that Marvin would try to turn Albert in for selling raw milk?"

Naomi shook her head. "I do not for a minute believe that Albert Yoder sold raw milk. It is against the law. And he is a good, law-abiding citizen. God-fearing."

"And the witnesses?" Cheryl asked.

"I do not think they are telling the truth."

Naomi's tone was so emphatic that Cheryl knew she believed every word she said. "So if they're not telling the truth, why are they lying?" That was the problem. Naomi could defend Albert Yoder until the proverbial cows came home, but the police had evidence.

"Well, if it is Marvin Chupp..." She allowed her sentence to trail off into nothing. It was one thing to imply that Marvin had set up Yoder and was lying about his involvement in selling raw milk and quite another altogether to say it out loud.

"I didn't think the Amish went in for such competition," Cheryl said. She had been around them enough to know that sport and games were high on their list of preferred activities, and these could get very competitive. She just hadn't realized that their competitive streak could reach out into other aspects of their lives.

"Amish or not," Naomi said, "he is still a person and very jealous of Albert Yoder's success."

Cheryl thought back to the farm that sat directly across the road from Albert Yoder's place. She couldn't tell a dime's worth of difference between the two, aside from the fact that Albert's farm was a total mess at the time. And she couldn't help but wonder if maybe Marvin Chupp had something to do with the rest of the Yoders' problems.

She shook the thought away. No reason to believe ill of Chupp, regardless of the problems he had with Albert. "I don't know, Naomi," Cheryl said. "We just have to trust the police in this matter."

"I do not think we have the luxury of waiting."

She was right. The Amish took care of most matters within the community, not always relying on the police. But that was because they forgave each other with such big hearts. Somehow, this was different.

"Please, Cheryl. I ask you as a friend."

It wasn't just the fate of Albert's milk, but a family of little girls who needed their father back, a baby on the way, and a wife who probably missed him very much as well. Cheryl felt herself cave before she even said the words. "Okay. On my lunch break I'll go down and talk to the chief."

Naomi wilted in relief. "Can I go too?"

"Why would you be in town at that time of day?"

"I think it is important for Rebekah. You may understand what the chief says and be able to explain it to me, but I will be able to explain it to Rebekah."

Cheryl couldn't argue with that logic. "Okay. At noon we'll go down together. Sound like a deal?"

Naomi stuck out her hand to shake. "Deal," she said with a satisfied smile.

Naomi showed up at twelve on the dot just as promised. That was how Cheryl found herself walking outside in the bright July sunshine on her way to figure out how to bail an Amish man out of jail.

"Who is that?" Naomi asked with a discreet nod off to the left.

Cheryl peered around at the latest newcomer to Sugarcreek. "Justin MacLean," she answered. She'd met the man just the other day.

"Oh," Naomi said.

Cheryl bit back a chuckle. She wouldn't want her friend to think she was laughing at her. But the look on her face was so shocked and filled with intrigue that Cheryl couldn't help it. She supposed there weren't many people around Sugarcreek like Justin MacLean. He was a hippie if she had ever seen one. Long hair and beard, bandanna around his neck. He couldn't even be called a hipster. Tie-dyed shirts, ratty blue jeans, and rope sandals on his feet. He carried a clipboard in one hand and stopped everybody who came past.

"What is he doing?" Naomi asked. "Running for city council?"

Cheryl didn't bother to remind Naomi that most city elections were held in November. "He's opened a new farm-to-table restaurant."

Naomi frowned. "What is 'farm-to-table'?"

Cheryl supposed that concept was as common to Naomi as it was uncommon to most English. The Amish just didn't call it by a certain phrase. "It's where the restaurant owns a farm and all the food they serve is straight from their farm to the table."

"Oh," Naomi said, but the confused frown still puckered her brow.

"It's a new concept for the English," Cheryl explained.

"Oh," Naomi said again. Cheryl could understand her confusion but didn't know what was the best way to explain it. Unlike the Amish, most English bought all their foodstuffs at the store. To the Amish, farm to table was just the norm.

"Why does he have a clipboard?"

Good question. "I don't know."

Naomi turned as they walked past on the opposite side of the street. She craned her head back for just a second and then trained her attention back to the front. They had more important matters to deal with this afternoon.

The dark-haired, bespectacled Delores sat behind the desk as usual. To her credit she didn't roll her eyes when she saw Naomi and Cheryl come into the office. Though Cheryl was beginning to suspect Delores had come up with her own code to let Chief Twitchell know just who it was when she came in.

"Is the chief here?" Cheryl asked.

"He's not." Delores smacked her gum and waited for Cheryl to continue.

"I need to find out about bond for Albert Yoder."

Delores shook her head then shuffled through some papers on her desk. "I believe they set the bond at a hundred thousand dollars."

Naomi gasped.

"A hundred thousand dollars?" Cheryl exclaimed. "For selling raw milk?"

Delores shook her head. "It's not up to me, but it seems that a lot of people are sick now and they blame Albert Yoder."

That Cheryl could understand, but a hundred thousand dollars? That meant raising ten thousand dollars to get him out of jail. "Are you aware that he has a pregnant wife who is about to give birth?"

Delores's face crumpled into an expression somewhat akin to compassion. "Yeah, I expect everybody around here knows that. But there's nothing I can do about that either. Or Chief Twitchell," she added before Cheryl could ask.

"Thank you," Cheryl said and led Naomi back out into the sunshine.

"What are we doing?" Naomi said. "Why did we leave?"

"We have to come up with a new plan," Cheryl explained. "The bond they set is so high. We'll need ten thousand dollars to get him out of jail."

Naomi stopped dead in her tracks. "So much! Why?"

Cheryl backtracked to where her friend stood. "I guess a lot of people are sick now because of the milk, and since they have witnesses, they feel they're fully justified keeping him in jail. I suppose they think that'll keep the milk from being sold." And if Albert Yoder was truly at fault, then it would, but like Naomi, Cheryl was beginning to have her doubts.

"There is one other thing," Naomi said. "The milk that was stolen illegally is the same milk that the Albert Yoders drink. None of them are sick."

"Do you think someone is tainting the milk in order to ruin Albert?" Cheryl asked.

"I do not know," Naomi replied.

But it was a possibility.

She glanced back down the street to where Justin MacLean stood with his clipboard and his tie-dyed shirt.

"So what do we do now?" Naomi asked.

"We get a bail bondsman."

Naomi started her feet back into motion. Cheryl walked next to her down the street. "A bail bondsman? What is that?"

"He'll help get Albert out of jail. He'll give Rebekah the money, and Albert just has to promise to stay in town until his court date."

"How generous!"

"Not really. See, she'll have to sign over her house or the farm, something as collateral."

Naomi was shaking her head before Cheryl was halfway finished speaking. "Amish do not do that."

Without a bondsman Albert Yoder was destined to stay in jail. She wasn't sure exactly how Amish Aid worked. But she had a feeling they couldn't use that much money just to get Albert Yoder out of jail.

That was something else she wasn't sure about. He was an Amish man and, as far as she knew, had no previous record. Even with several people claiming illnesses, it seemed excessive. So why such a steep bond?

Thoughts of Albert Yoder, raw milk, and poor pregnant Rebekah plagued Cheryl throughout the rest of the afternoon. Naomi went back to the farm to help Levi with the alpaca and get her own chores completed while Cheryl spent the afternoon helping tourists find just the right Amish souvenir to take back home.

At six o'clock on the dot she locked up the Swiss Miss, placed Beau in his carrier, and started for her house.

"Miss, will you sign this?"

Justin MacLean shoved the clipboard underneath Cheryl's nose.

She took a step back. "What's this for?"

MacLean smiled as if it were the very question he had been waiting for. "I own the new farm-to-table restaurant. It's down off Cypress Road. We serve fresh food. All organic and this is a petition to allow us to sell raw milk in the county."

Cheryl shook her head. She had done enough research to know. "But the sale of raw milk is illegal in the entire state of Ohio." And as far as she knew, that included Tuscarawas County.

"Are you a registered voter with the county?"

Cheryl wasn't, but she wouldn't tell him that. Not yet. Something about Justin MacLean made the little hairs on the back of her neck stand on end. Plus, too much was being said about raw milk these days, and she couldn't help but believe that it was more than a coincidence. "Why is the sale of raw milk so important to you?" she asked instead.

"Unprocessed milk is the way God intended for it to be consumed."

Cheryl didn't bother to explain to him cows' milk was meant for baby cows and really not for human consumption at all. She wanted to find out more from the man, not alienate him completely.

She took the clipboard and started to read the petition at the top.

"It's pretty straightforward," MacLean explained. "I believe the government shouldn't interfere so much with the choice of consumption. If someone wants to use raw milk in a recipe or drink it straight, then who is the government to say that they can't? You get my drift?"

Cheryl handed the petition back to him. "Yeah, I get it. But I'm sorry, I'm not a registered voter here." She'd set up residence in Sugarcreek, but voting was one thing she hadn't thought about during the few months she'd been here. Not that she would sign MacLean's petition if she had. Not standing in the middle of the street anyway. This sort of decision required some thought. And raw milk wasn't something she thought about every day.

Still, there was something about the man that made her want to talk to him, something that made her think there was more to this deal with Albert Yoder than simply Marvin Chupp and an age-old competition.

MacLean reached into his back pocket and pulled out a creased white business card with bold green letters. Chicken Pluck, it read. The name alone was enough to turn most people off, but she kept reading. *The restaurant of the future. All organic, farm-to-table. Call for reservations. Dinner service begins at five,* with a phone number underneath. "I hope you'll come visit. Really good food. I do all the cooking myself."

"So you're not open for lunch?"

"I hope to eventually. But until we get everything rolling, we're just serving an evening meal."

Cheryl gave a small nod. Soon she would go over and check out the Chicken Pluck. She might even eat there if she could get over the name. And with any luck, she just might find out a thing or two about this raw-milk situation.

Her thoughts tumbled one on top of another as she cooked her dinner, which consisted of heating up a microwave meal and pouring herself a glass of iced tea. In the months since she and Lance had parted ways, she had become accustomed to the differences in her life now. She loved being in Sugarcreek, and she loved running the Swiss Miss. But there were times when it seemed that so much was happening at one time and that her thoughts were spinning faster than she could grab hold of them. She needed someone to talk to, a sounding board. Beau would have to do right now.

He blinked his blue eyes at her balefully as he watched her eat in front of the TV.

"What do you think?" she asked the kitty.

He didn't even bother to meow in return, simply licked one paw, swiped it across his face, and laid his head down once again.

"See there's this problem with raw milk," she told the sleeping cat. One ear twitched, but other than that he didn't move.

"Well, it's more than just about raw milk. It seems there are all sorts of things going on at the Yoder farm. Someone's been releasing the horses, and someone has torn up all the hay. Somebody crashed into the barn, and who knows if that was an accident or not? And then there's the broken water pipe, the manure, and a malicious neighbor. Not to mention a new restaurant owner who wants to buy raw milk and a dairy farmer in jail for selling raw milk. Everything is a jumbled-up mess."

Somehow it was all connected...somewhere. Her thoughts continued to tumble over themselves. If she could just figure out which one to grab on to, she might be able to straighten the whole thing out. But which one?

Naomi had set her sights on Marvin Chupp. Cheryl had to admit that he looked a little too happy to see his neighbor led away in handcuffs, though Cheryl supposed that having to deal with mud and manure on the road on a daily basis might prove more than most neighbors could deal with. But would he really go over and steal Albert's milk? And perhaps poison it to ruin the other man? And how exactly did one steal milk? She still hadn't figured that out.

Maybe she should run out and talk to Rebekah on Monday, just take a little extra lunchtime and check on the poor woman. Swing by maybe and pick up Naomi. All in the interest of being a good neighbor.

Maybe then she could even talk to Marvin Chupp a little more and see what he knew. Maybe he heard somebody steal the milk or maybe even set the horses free?

Cheryl gathered up her tray and carried it back to the kitchen. "Don't mind me," she told Beau.

He twitched his tail as she walked past but otherwise feigned sleep.

There was just so much. Too many things unexplained, too many things that were almost connected but not. And there was just something about Justin MacLean that didn't sit quite right with her. What difference would it make if they could sell milk in the county if it was a state law? That just didn't make sense. Or maybe his skills didn't stretch past the kitchen, and, poli-sci wasn't his strong suit.

She just couldn't help but think that Justin MacLean had something to do with the milk disappearing. And that Marvin Chupp was bound and determined to keep Albert Yoder in jail.

Unfortunately until she figured out the connection, that was just where he would remain.

CHAPTER THREE

At noon on Monday, Cheryl hopped into her car as she promised herself and headed out to get Naomi. She mulled over the problem half the night but couldn't come up with any plausible explanation for the bizarre happenings at the Yoder farm.

Or maybe she was trying to make them all come from one source and they were coming from several. Who was to say that a group of ornery teenagers weren't the ones releasing the horses while someone else completely different was stealing the milk? After all, why would someone be so against one man to cause all these problems for him? It just didn't make sense.

As usual, the Miller farm was a flurry of activity. Seth was repairing fences and gates at the petting zoo area, while Caleb made sure that the animals remained inside their pens. Chickens pecked the ground, cats wandered around, and Rover lay in the shade. It was the perfect picture of a busy summer day on an Amish farm. And the sight of it brought a smile to Cheryl's lips.

As she pulled up, Seth looked up from his work and gave her a small wave.

Cheryl returned it and started for the house, hoping that Naomi had gotten the message about going over to visit with Rebekah today.

Cheryl had a small stab of conscience about "visiting" with Rebekah. More than anything she wanted to visit with Marvin Chupp. Maybe he had seen something more than he was telling. It was worth a shot to ask.

Cheryl opened the screen door and poked her head inside. "Naomi? Are you ready?"

Naomi came bustling down the stairs, no shoes as usual, her bare feet barely making a sound on the wood floor. "I am. Just give me one more second to get the laundry off the line."

Cheryl had heard so many people say that the Amish did all their laundry on Monday, but with a family the size of Naomi's, it seemed as if she did laundry all the time.

Elizabeth came out of the kitchen with the dust rag in one hand and a can of furniture polish in the other. "I will get the laundry, Maam."

"I thought you were going to dust for me," Naomi said.

"I can do both." Elizabeth smiled.

"Thank you, Daughter." Naomi turned to Cheryl. "I guess I am ready to go then."

Cheryl palmed her keys, and together she and Naomi headed for the car.

"How much laundry do you have to do?" Cheryl asked as they started down the road toward the Yoder farm.

Naomi shook her head. "You have no idea. There is always laundry. Thankfully we do not have to iron as much as we used to. But it seems like with seven of us in the house the laundry just never stops."

"I can only imagine." And to think that Naomi did it all with her wringer washer. Then she hung it on the line to dry and took it down the next day. Just in time to start another load to hang up all over again.

"How much laundry do you think Rebekah Yoder has to do?"

"More than any one person should have to," was Naomi's response.

Cheryl chuckled and turned her car into the driveway at the Yoders' house.

As it had been in previous visits, chaos seemed to be the underlying theme of the farm. The water still bubbled up from a broken pipe, and Cheryl couldn't figure out why no one could get it turned off or repaired. Or maybe they just broke another one. Who knew? Cows bellowed from the pasture, seemingly uncomfortable with so many people milling around, construction workers and surveyors. Even a couple of men in suits and hard hats picked their way through the muddy yard.

Naomi took one look around and sighed. "It is a mess."

Cheryl had to agree. The whole farm was still a mess. How did one man have so many trials in such a short period of time?

The front door opened, and Abigail Yoder poked her head out to see who was visiting. Her eyes widened with excitement. "Naomi! Cheryl! Come in, come in." She opened the door and stood holding it for them to enter the house. Cheryl's steps faltered. True, she had said that she was coming out to check on Rebekah, but in truth her neighbor was really Cheryl's target.

"You go on, Naomi. I want to go talk to Marvin Chupp." She nodded toward the house across the road.

Naomi frowned and gave her head a slight shake. "You want me to go with you?" Her tone clearly said, "Please say no."

"No," Cheryl said. "You go check on Rebekah. I only have a little time before I need to get back to the shop."

Naomi expelled a small sigh then turned and started toward the house.

Cheryl stood where she was until Naomi and Abigail had gone back into the house. Then she crossed her arms and surveyed the farm before her.

If anything, it looked worse than it had the last time they were there. Maybe because the water had been leaking on the ground for who knew how long. It had started to form little puddles. And Cheryl was afraid that if they didn't get it stopped, the Yoders would end up having a beach in place of the barn.

She didn't understand why someone didn't simply turn off the water at the source, but who was she to say? They needed to do something. That was for sure.

Cheryl turned as a heavyset woman started across the road between the two houses. She wore an olive green dress and a black apron, the kerchief on her head cut from the same material. Like Naomi and Abigail, she was barefoot, seemingly unfazed by the heat of the pavement or any of the rocks she encountered on her way across the road.

"Hi," Cheryl said. She had truly come to talk to Marvin Chupp, but it seemed that maybe his wife was just as good of a choice.

"Are you friends of the Yoders?" the woman asked. She glanced over her shoulder as if waiting for someone to call her back. She quickly turned back around to Cheryl.

"I suppose, yes."

The woman thrust a plastic laundry basket full of clothes toward Cheryl. "These are not mine. From the look of the size of the things, they belong to the Yoders. Could you give them to Rebekah for me?"

"We just came for a quick visit. Why don't you come in and . . ."

"Oh, I cannot do that." The woman shook her head.

"I'm Cheryl Cooper." She stuck out her hand to shake. In the few months that she had been in Sugarcreek, she had learned that the Amish weren't very big on introductions, but she liked knowing whom she was talking to.

The woman shook it quickly as if time was of the essence. "Nellie Chupp."

"Nice to meet you."

Nellie nodded but didn't return the sentiment. Another thing Cheryl was becoming accustomed to as one of the Amish idiosyncrasies.

"I'll ask Rebekah about these clothes," Cheryl said.

"I must get back," Nellie said. She headed across the road, and Cheryl started behind her.

"Can you talk for a minute? I have a couple of questions about…"

The woman waved a hand behind her head as she continued to march toward her house. "Not a good time."

Cheryl stopped as Nellie waddled back across the road. The front door opened, and Nellie practically ran back to her own laundry line.

"Nellie," Marvin called from the porch. "Where have you been?"

"Right here, Husband," Nellie lied.

Marvin said something in Dutch that was lost on Cheryl.

Nellie replied, and just like that the exchange was over.

Marvin went down the steps and across the yard. At first Cheryl thought he might be coming over to talk, but then she realized he was just positioning himself to get a better view of the chaos at the Yoder farm.

Cheryl supposed that if she wasn't happy with her neighbor, something like this would be quite entertaining to watch. But that still didn't explain what Marvin Chupp had against Albert Yoder or why.

She waved toward Marvin, hoping to gain his attention. He ignored her for about as long as he could, so she called out to him. "Marvin Chupp."

Almost involuntarily, his head swung around and his gaze caught hers.

She smiled. "Can I ask you something?"

The man pressed his lips together and shook his head, but Cheryl wasn't about to be dissuaded. She looked both ways and started across the road.

"So you've not heard anything out of the ordinary at night?"

Marvin frowned at her. "I do not know what you mean."

Cheryl realized how awkward her question sounded. She tried again. "You've not heard anything at night over at the Yoder's that sounded suspicious? Only the usual?"

"That is right," Marvin said.

"No other sounds? You know, like the horses getting out or the hay being destroyed?"

Marvin crossed his arms as if to shut her out of the conversation. "I do not recall."

"What about the salt in the garden? Do you know anything about who could've put salt on Rebekah's tomatoes?"

"No." The one word was meant to cut off any remainder of their conversation, but Cheryl was not about to be put aside so quickly.

"Would you tell me if you heard anything?"

His gaze met hers, and Cheryl could see the decades of animosity flickering there. She wouldn't put anything past Marvin Chupp, not with feelings like that hovering just below the surface.

"Why should I, *Englisch*?" he said, and behind him his wife gasped.

He seemed not to care that he had been rude beyond measure. Instead, he turned on one heel and marched back to the house. He slammed the door shut, leaving both Cheryl and Nellie staring after him.

Cheryl was about go back across the road when Nellie waved and caught her attention. "Do you see that phone shanty right there?" Nellie asked.

Cheryl nodded. They had passed the shanty on the way in. The small white shack sat on the side of the road, a little house to shelter the phone. The Amish used them in lieu of having phones in their houses. Cheryl supposed this one was shared by the Chupps and the Yoders and perhaps even one more family, and she had to wonder how Marvin felt about sharing the phone with Albert. It might get pretty interesting around there on heavy call days.

"Meet me there," Nellie said, her voice dropping to nearly a whisper. "Give me ten minutes."

Cheryl nodded, all the while trying to act as if she weren't talking to Nellie. She wouldn't want the woman's husband to get up in arms before she found out what was on the woman's mind.

Ten minutes seemed to be an eternity. Cheryl walked around the car, visually checked the tire pressure, and kicked one tire just a smidge to see if it had enough air in it. She noticed she had a small nick in her windshield, probably from some truck throwing a rock on it. And there was a tiny scratch on the passenger side door, which meant she had probably taken a shopping cart to the flank. Still, she loved her little blue car.

She tried not to watch and see when Nellie wandered away from her laundry and entered the phone shanty. And she could only hope that Marvin wasn't watching as she slipped inside the little building behind her. It was a tight fit, but Cheryl had a feeling it would be well worth it.

"You have something you want to tell me?" Cheryl asked.

Nellie nodded. "People have been coming in and out all hours of the night. But I do not think it is Albert Yoder."

"Why not?"

"They were here last night. How could that be Albert? Wasn't he in jail?"

"Good point." Cheryl wished there was a little bit more light in the place, but there was only a single window that let in some sunshine. They both tried to stay away from it in case Marvin happened to look out the window and over to the phone shanty. The last thing she needed was to get Nellie in trouble for talking to her. But she wished she could read her features as they talked.

"Have vehicles been waking you up as well?"

"From time to time I suppose, but I never can see anything when I look out the window. Of course Marvin won't let me come over and check things out, and he is not coming over. Men and their feuds."

Cheryl nodded in agreement as if she understood, but in reality she had never known any feud to go on so long. She couldn't help but wonder if either man could even remember what it was all about. She hadn't heard anyone say what started the original argument, just that they engaged in competition regularly to best the other.

"What about the barn?" Cheryl asked.

"What about it?"

"Do you think someone is stealing the milk from the barn? Do you think that the same person knocked the barn down?"

Nellie shook her head. "Oh no, I saw the barn fall, and that was definitely due to the big bulldozer thing that is over there. The driver was not paying attention and backed into it at the corner. I guess he hit it just right and the whole thing came tumbling down. It is probably time for a new barn when something like that happens."

"I guess," Cheryl said, though she had no idea.

"So do you think the people who are coming to the farm at night are the people who are stealing the milk?"

"I do not know anything about missing milk," Nellie said. "All I can tell you is that from time to time I find their clothes lying in my yard. I hear things at night, but I cannot see what is going on, and I am not sure I want to know."

That Cheryl could understand. "What about your farm? Have you been missing milk? Have any of your clothes disappeared?"

Once again, Nellie shook her head. "Every now and then we end up with a little bit of teenager mischief, but that is what happens when you have a fourteen-year-old." She smiled.

Cheryl returned it, wondering exactly what sort of trouble fourteen-year-old Amish kids got into. She bet it didn't compare in volumes or severity to most English kids. And for that, most Amish families should be grateful.

"And the laundry just shows up on the lawn?" Cheryl asked.

"Sometimes it just appears on my laundry line. Sometimes on the ground. I always rewash them. I have been hanging on to them until I had a chance to return them."

Cheryl looked down at the basket of clothing she still held in her arms. She set it on the shelf someone had hammered on to the wall at one end of the shanty. She started looking through it. There was no rhyme or reason to the clothing or why it should all be lumped together. Some dresses were small and obviously belonged to Gracie, the youngest of the Yoder girls. There were a couple more in different sizes, a few pair of unmentionables, along with various towels.

"Any of this show up today?"

Nellie shook her head. "Oh no, I have been collecting this for a couple of weeks."

Cheryl looked at the clothes again. "Was it hanging on the line?"

"No. Sometimes it was just lying in the yard, and other times it was on the porch."

That was still strange.

"How do you suppose it got there?"

Nellie shrugged. "I guess Rebekah does not pin her laundry good enough, though here lately it has been the girls doing it."

Another strike against the girls and the completion of their chores. Cheryl hadn't spent a great deal of time with the Yoder girls, but what she had seen of them was that they were as hardworking as any. They seemed to care about their family and taking responsibility for their family's farm. Just like Naomi's children. They might not be perfect, after all they were kids. Still, Amish teens for the most part carried their own weight and did things right. At least more so than the average English kid as far as she could tell.

"Thank you for returning these. I'll make sure that Rebekah gets them."

Nellie smiled. "I am glad at times like these that she has good friends like you."

The sentiment warmed Cheryl's heart. She hadn't thought about being a good friend to anyone other than Naomi, but she liked the Yoders, and she hated that they were having such trouble. And again, despite all the grumpiness of her husband, Cheryl liked Nellie Chupp. "Me too."

She turned to the door of the phone shanty, laundry basket tucked under one arm, then turned back to Nellie. "Why do Marvin and Albert hate each other so much?"

Nellie pressed her lips together and shook her head. "I do not really know. Marvin refuses to talk about it. He refuses to let me be friends with Rebekah. I would love to help out from time to time. My youngest is fourteen," Nellie said. "I have more time on my hands than I did before, and I would love to give her a neighborly hand from time to time. But Marvin will not hear of it."

Cheryl mentally calculated the age difference between Albert and Marvin and figured they could have been in school together. Though she felt like Marvin was a bit older.

"I understand," Cheryl said as she slipped out of the shanty.

Behind her she heard Nellie mutter, "Really? Because I do not."

Cheryl walked back to their neighbor's house without looking back. If Marvin was watching all of the goings-on at the Yoder farm, she sure didn't want it to show that she had been talking to Nellie.

Despite the fact that Cheryl knew it was a common practice, she still had a hard time just walking into the Yoders' house. So she gave a quick knock and stepped inside. "Rebekah? Naomi?"

"In here," Naomi returned.

Having been in once before, Cheryl easily made her way to the kitchen where Naomi and Rebekah sat at the table.

"What have you got there?" Rebekah asked.

Cheryl jerked a thumb over her shoulder back toward the direction of the Chupp house. "It was sort of strange, but Nellie Chupp came over and gave me this basket of clothes to give you."

"Basket of clothes?"

Cheryl nodded. "It seems that they blew into her yard. Or perhaps someone dropped them there."

"My clothes? My family's clothes?" Rebekah asked.

"Apparently," Cheryl said. "She said she would find them from time to time, and Marvin wouldn't let her bring them over. So she rewashed them and waited for an opportunity. I guess she thought I was a safe bet, so she came over and gave them to me."

Naomi looked from Cheryl to Rebekah. "I guess that explains the missing clothing."

But there were still a lot of other mysterious happenings on the Yoder farm besides just missing clothes. It didn't explain the salt on her tomatoes, and it didn't explain their horses getting loose. The events could all be tied together or individual incidences. Who knew?

Rebekah started to stand, but Naomi waved her back, hopping to her feet and taking the basket from Cheryl. She set it on the table and started rummaging through it. "What else is missing?" she asked.

Rebekah leaned back and folded her hands over her large belly. Cheryl couldn't imagine how uncomfortable she had to feel, and she wondered how much longer Rebekah really had before the baby arrived. "Let's see, I know there were two of Gracie's dresses missing."

Naomi dug around until she found the two garments, one blue, one yellow, and laid them neatly on top of each other on one end of the table.

"One of Albert's shirts and two pairs of his pants."

Naomi continued to dig then stopped. "I don't see those in here. What else?"

"Two of our church aprons and one of my dresses along with a bunch of other things. Dish towels, underwear of all things, even bath towels."

Naomi shuffled the clothes around, rattling off the inventory as she did so. "It looks like there are some undergarments in here, plus two bath towels, no wait—three bath towels, a washcloth, a dish towel, and what appears to be a pot holder."

Rebekah nodded. "Gracie spilled grape jelly on the pot holder, and I threw it in the laundry. I forgot about that."

"How long ago was that?" Cheryl asked.

Rebekah shrugged. "Maybe a month ago?" She seemed to think about it a second. "No, it could have only been about two weeks ago."

Two weeks. How long had things been going crazy at the Yoder farm? Longer than that, she was sure.

Naomi folded the clothes back to rights and stacked them neatly in the basket. "Well, at least she got most of your clothes back, right?"

Rebekah nodded. "I guess I should take her basket back to her tomorrow."

Cheryl shook her head. "She said not to. I think she doesn't want Marvin to know that she was talking to you."

Rebekah pressed her lips together much in the same way that Nellie had when talking about the feud between their husbands. "I just don't understand it."

"Do you know what started it?" Cheryl asked.

Rebekah rubbed a hand over her belly as if soothing the kicking baby then shook her head. "Albert will not talk about it. The minute I bring up Marvin, he clams up worse than anything. He will not listen to me or talk to me about it, and he surely will not tell me what happened. It must have been really bad for him to be so tight-lipped about it."

Naomi nodded. "Amish men are not known to hold a grudge, but they are human after all."

All Cheryl could do was nod. Yes, the Amish were known for forgiveness. But one thing she had learned since she had been living in Sugarcreek was that they were people, just people. They had feelings and battled internal issues. They had health problems and personality conflicts. They had arguments, bad times, and good times. Why should it be unheard of that two Amish men were embedded in a feud? As much is it seemed to go against everything the Amish stood for, it still was part of human nature. But what could take two men who had once been friends and turn them into bitter enemies?

Cheryl mulled the question over, wondering if that had anything to do with the missing milk or if it was merely a coincidence.

"There are really no fireworks in town tonight?" Cheryl looked from Seth to Naomi and back to Levi and started the trip all over again. Each one of them appeared serious. But how could that be?

"You're in the little Switzerland of Ohio," Seth said by way of explanation. "We celebrate Switzerland's independence."

"And you have fireworks then?" Cheryl asked.

"Oh ja," Levi said. "It's a big celebration."

"And that's in August?" Cheryl reiterated.

Naomi nodded.

"But you're still in America," Cheryl protested. "Why not have one now too?"

The look on all three faces was so incredulous that Cheryl had to bite back a laugh.

"Everybody has a Fourth of July celebration," Naomi said. "What is the novelty in that?"

"That is right," Seth chimed in. "Besides, you can drive over to Dover if you want to see fireworks that badly."

"Or drive out to the clay pit," Levi chimed in.

There was a large brick factory there in Sugarcreek. It sat next to a clay pit where the clay was mined and then turned into bricks. Cheryl had been meaning to get out there since she had come to Sugarcreek, but just had never managed to. She'd never been to a brick factory before or even a clay mine for that matter. She thought it would be interesting to check it out.

"So what's at the clay pit?"

"Oh, it is a great place to shoot off fireworks because you do not have to worry about anything catching fire out there."

"You want to go?" Naomi asked.

Just then Eli walked into the room. "Go where?"

"Out to the clay pit to shoot off fireworks," Cheryl said. "Is that what you do for fun on the Fourth of July?"

"Can we go? I've never been." Eli's eyes were wide and excited. "Please! It will be fun."

"I think that will be up to your mom and dad," Cheryl said diplomatically. She wasn't sure how much fun it would be to go buy a few fireworks and shoot them off in the middle of nowhere. But fireworks were tricky. Some people liked to shoot them off, and some people liked to watch them. Others preferred to stay as far away from them as they could because of the noise.

"Is that why you don't have a show here? Because the noise scares the horses?" Cheryl asked. "No wait," she said remembering that they lit fireworks in August on the Swiss national holiday. "Forget I said that."

"If you want to go out to Dover," Naomi said, "they have a big show there. It is not so far away."

No, Dover wasn't far, just about ten minutes down the road. But it made her a little sad to think that she wasn't going to be in Sugarcreek itself for the Fourth of July. She pushed those thoughts away.

"What if we all go out to the quarry?" Eli asked. "I heard some people say they were going to take a fire pit down there and roast some marshmallows. It sounds like a lot of fun."

"You sure it's okay to shoot fireworks off there?" Cheryl asked. Not that she particularly cared to light up a bunch of explosives, but it would be a different way of spending the Fourth of July. And it certainly would be something that she could only do in Sugarcreek.

Cheryl wasn't sure what to expect when she pulled up to the clay pit that evening just before dark. But she certainly hadn't expected a large bonfire with people milling about, a roped-off section for firework-safe play, and tents and booths galore.

She parked in the graveled lot off to one side, and everyone piled out. Naomi had insisted on coming, and for that Cheryl was grateful. Otherwise she didn't think any of them would have come. It was just the four of them—Naomi and Seth along with Cheryl and Eli. Levi had stayed behind, citing some work that had to be completed by the morning, and Caleb, Elizabeth, and Esther just weren't interested.

Naomi looked around and frowned. "Are you sure this is safe?"

"It will be fine," Seth said and went around to the trunk of the car and waited for Cheryl to open it.

They had gone out to the highway and bought a few fireworks to set off. Eli grabbed them and then spotted someone he knew. He seemed like a kid tonight, way more excited than any one person should be about setting off firecrackers.

"Be careful," his mother called after him.

She turned back to Cheryl and shook her head. "The things you get me into."

Cheryl hooked her arm through Naomi's and laughed. "Come on. There are marshmallows over there."

Together they walked toward the bonfire, Seth close behind. More than anything Cheryl was looking forward to just enjoying an evening of fun. It seemed like every day had been filled with something or another from arrest to accusations to just everyday work. A little bit of relaxation was exactly what they needed.

"Seth!" A tall man came toward them. His hand extended, and a big smile was on his face. "I didn't expect to see you here."

Seth smiled and shook the man's hand. "Eli wanted to come out and shoot off fireworks."

"Well, enjoy yourselves. All the money raised here tonight is going to the Schrock boy."

Seth nodded, and the man moved away.

"What's the matter with the Schrock boy?" Cheryl asked.

Seth shook his head. "It is the saddest thing. He has leukemia."

"And the money they raise here tonight will go toward his treatment?" Cheryl asked. She had attended a couple of benefit auctions since she had been in Sugarcreek. Yet this was a little bit different.

"Ja," Naomi said.

"Seems to be a good way to raise money." That was one thing Cheryl had always admired about the Amish. They were always taking care of each other. "How does it work exactly?" Cheryl asked.

Seth frowned. "Everyone here has donated their time and the food. All the money they bring in will go directly to the family. That way they'll have extra to put toward their child's treatment."

"On top of Amish Aid?"

"Ja, though in a situation like this, it is hard to say how much Amish Aid will be able to pay for the family. That's why we have auctions."

Cheryl looked at all the people in attendance. Most had some sort of food or drink in their hands. Someone had even brought out a popcorn machine, and that was in addition to the marshmallows and all of the other goodies that were available to roast in the bonfire. It was a perfect setup, really. People were out here, they needed to be fed, and a young boy needed treatment. It seemed a match made in heaven.

"Let's go get something to eat. I can't think of a better reason to eat a hot dog than to help a little boy who has leukemia."

Chapter Four

It wasn't really the smartest idea she'd had to see if perhaps Sugarcreek's newest newcomer had something to do with the Yoders' milk disappearing, but it would be fun to go to a new restaurant and try it out.

Cheryl got out of her car on Tuesday and walked to the front door of Chicken Pluck. Maybe eventually she would be able to get past the name...

It smelled heavenly inside, or maybe she was just hungry from skipping lunch. But she would grab a quick bite to eat and take a really good look at the menu, then maybe she'd be able to see if perhaps the owner had more than his fair share of an obsession over raw milk.

The inside of the Chicken Pluck was rustic; this certainly made it feel more like a farm. But she had read up online about some of these farm-to-table restaurants where the restaurant building itself actually sat on the farm. This one sat just down the road. She had asked around and found out that MacLean had bought the English farm and was now using it to grow his produce. If nothing else, she supposed she could chalk this one up to being healthy, organic, and all that. That was if she could find a place to sit.

She'd barely found a place to park. This sort of restaurant was a new concept to Sugarcreek, and from the looks of the crowd standing in the foyer, it was well on its way to being a major hit. Though she secretly wondered how many of the people waiting to dine thought the place was Amish-owned.

That was one thing she'd learned right off. Amish-owned businesses usually didn't put the word *Amish* in the title. More often than not, the establishment had only the name for the shopper to go by . . . like, Schrock's Seeds. But since this had neither, it was really anybody's guess.

She eased her way to the front counter, where a young man in a gingham shirt and a pair of jeans waited for her. All he needed was a rope belt to complete his Jethro Clampett look, but she wasn't casting stones. MacLean had done everything in his power to make the place feel homey, country, and like the diner had stepped back to the farm.

"Hi. I just need an order to go."

The man shook his head. "I'd like to say we can have that out for you in a jiffy, but it's been a little busier than we thought and we're not able to do to-go orders right now."

Cheryl looked at the many people standing around.

"We're hoping to be able to have a to-go order window and everything set up soon, but . . . " He shrugged and let his words trail off, and Cheryl decided the ending.

That was okay, she thought. She really wanted a gander at the menu more than anything.

"Do you have a to-go menu or even just a menu I can take with me to look over for when I want to come back to eat?"

The guy handed her a sheet of paper that looked something like parchment paper. Or maybe onion skin. It had what appeared to be a handwritten menu on it, though she was sure it had been photocopied for the occasion.

"This is tonight's menu."

Cheryl frowned. "What do you mean tonight's menu? I don't understand."

He gave her an indulgent smile. No doubt he'd had to explain this very thing countless times before. "Our restaurant is centered around food availability."

"Huh?"

His smile tightened. "We grow the food for the table at the farm. Some things will get ripe and others won't. We'll run out of things from time to time. So we won't know what's on each day's menu until that day."

It was a really unique concept, she had to admit. But that didn't help her any in trying to figure out if MacLean was responsible for stealing Yoder's milk. It was probably a wash anyway, but it would've been fun to come and eat.

"We're taking reservations for next week. I could put you down a week from tomorrow. Say at seven thirty?"

And he was good at his job. "Sure. That'd be great."

He cast a pointed look behind her then trained his gaze back to her. "Party of one?"

"Better make that two." Maybe not the most mature thing she had ever said, but there was something in his attitude that made her want him to know she had people to dine with.

He penciled her in, gave her a card. "This is the part where I invite you to come out to the farm and have a look around. Most people like to come out the same day as their reservation."

Cheryl shook her head. "Are you serious?"

"Unfortunately, yes."

Why unfortunately? "And what would I do at the farm?" she asked.

"Justin opens it so that people can get a true feel of the food that they're eating. You'll be able to see the fields where he grows the food. We have taste testing for the fresh veggies and games for the children."

Cheryl didn't bother to tell him that she didn't have any children. She just nodded politely as he handed her the pamphlet outlining the open-house times of the farm and let herself out of the restaurant. She headed toward her car in the jam-packed parking lot, mulling over the turn of events. Maybe she would invite Naomi to come with her. That would be fun. Naomi didn't get out nearly enough as far as Cheryl was concerned. But she knew that was the Amish way. Naomi cooked every night for her family. And she was very good at it. But it would be a treat for her to be able to come out to a restaurant, sit down, and have someone wait on her for a change.

And if she was really lucky, she would persuade Naomi to go out to the Chicken Pluck Farm and poke around. As up in arms as her friend was concerning the problems the Yoders were having, Cheryl didn't think it would take much convincing to get her out to MacLean's farm. While they were there, if they just happened to uncover a few clues as to MacLean's intentions, all the better.

"Have you thought any more about what we can do to get Albert Yoder out of jail?" Naomi asked that Thursday morning.

Albert Yoder had been in jail for days, without any success in trying to get him out. It seemed the state of Ohio took Listeria seriously.

Cheryl shook her head. "Aside from getting a bail bondsman, I don't know what to do."

Naomi gave a stern nod. "We need to have a benefit auction."

"A benefit auction?"

"Ja, the community donates items. Then everyone gets together, and we auction them off."

"What kind of items?" Cheryl asked.

Naomi shrugged. "Anything, really. Quilts, farm equipment, cases of jelly, applesauce, it can be anything as long as it is of use to someone else. And pretty much everything is."

That was true, especially where the Amish were concerned. Everything was of some use to someone. "I think that's a great idea. How do we get started?"

Naomi smiled. "You just leave that up to me. I will get everything going. I will talk to the Amish people and get donations from them. Would you...?" She dropped her gaze then shyly lifted it back to Cheryl's. "Could you ask the Englisch merchants to maybe donate some things?"

"Of course," Cheryl said. "I'll even donate some stuff myself." She could donate things from the Swiss Miss as well as some of the things she had in storage in Columbus. Of course that would mean a trip back to get them, but it was for a good cause.

"Oh, that would be *wunderbar goot*," Naomi said. "We will have Albert Yoder out of jail in no time."

But raising ten thousand dollars was not going to be easy, Cheryl thought. Naomi had left that morning with a lightened step as she pulled her empty wagon behind her and out the door of the Swiss Miss. She said she was going to check on the Yoders and see how everything was out at the farm. She acted as if it were the first time she'd been out there, but Cheryl had a feeling she'd been visiting every day. Most likely more than once, to check on the Yoder women. So far Rebekah Yoder hadn't gone into labor yet. But it was only a matter of time. And Cheryl would love it if they could get Albert out of jail before then. The man deserved to see his child born. No matter that he had six others. Every birth was a miracle, and he needed to be there for it.

She went about her morning doing the usual things. The bus driver brought in a load of tourists who wiped her completely out of strawberry jam and quilt-top pot holders. One thing was certain: business at the Swiss Miss was booming. And for that she should be grateful.

Lydia Troyer came in at three, and after giving her a few instructions, Cheryl grabbed her wallet and headed out the door. Her plan was simple: walk down the street in one direction, stop at every store and ask for donations, tell them why, and see what she could rustle up. Then she would swing around the other side and make a big circle, ending up back at the Swiss Miss. But after about three stores, she was starting to sweat. It was hotter than anything out here.

She went into the pawnshop, wishing she had made a note as to all the stores where she stopped. Most needed to wait on their owner to come back or said they would have to think about what they could donate before they committed. But everyone seemed interested in helping Albert Yoder. As far as she knew he was an upstanding citizen of Sugarcreek. And he didn't deserve to be in jail any more than she did. But that nagging thought of witnesses stayed with her as she walked over to the counter.

"Cheryl," Wendy greeted her. "Good to see you."

Cheryl gave a quick nod. "You too." Despite their rocky start from last Christmas, Wendy had become a valuable member of the Sugarcreek community. Cheryl really couldn't say a friend, but she was glad to see Wendy and her son Drake had stayed in the area. Even though their shop looked so temporary during the holidays. "I've come about a serious matter today, Wendy." She waited until she had the woman's full attention before she continued. "Albert Yoder, the dairy farmer, has been arrested."

"I heard something about that," Wendy said.

"Well, Naomi Miller and I are trying to get together a benefit auction for him. He's got a baby on the way, and we're trying to get him out of jail before his wife goes into labor. I was hoping maybe you could donate something to the auction on his behalf."

"Of course, of course. Let me look and see what I've got. Can I get back to you tomorrow?"

Cheryl nodded. It had been that way all over. She'd have to make another trip around tomorrow and see if she could collect the promises and pledges.

But Sugarcreek was a great little community, and she was certain everyone would back up their word without hesitation.

"That'd be just fine, Wendy. I appreciate it a lot. And the Yoders do too."

Wendy smiled. "That's what neighbors are for."

With those words rattling around in her head, Cheryl stepped out into the July sunlight and made her way toward the Swiss Miss. She was hot and thirsty and could use a snack.

The thought crossed her mind just as she got to the Honey Bee Café. Perfect.

She pushed open the door and stepped inside the cool interior of the quaint little café. If truth be known, she enjoyed the Honey Bee much more than a person should enjoy an eating establishment. But there was just something about the place with its quaint atmosphere, healthy foods, and sunny take on everything.

"Hey there, Cheryl Cooper," Kathy Snyder said. She was the owner of the Honey Bee and had become fast friends with Cheryl since she'd been in town. "What brings you in today? Or maybe I should say at this time of day?" Cheryl loved to come eat lunch. But coming in at three thirty in the afternoon was not her normal MO.

"I've been out collecting for a benefit auction for Albert Yoder."

Kathy pressed her lips together in a small frown. "I heard about that. It's just tragic."

"I know. Naomi Miller is very concerned. Especially about Rebekah Yoder."

Kathy gave another nod. "So I take it she hasn't had her baby yet?"

"Not yet but it's going to be anytime now. And we would like to get Albert out of jail before the baby comes."

"That'd be best, huh? Can I get you something to eat?"

Cheryl ordered a bagel and a Diet Coke then took her snack to a little table to sit down. She hadn't been there more than five minutes before Kathy joined her once again.

"Going to stick your nose in the newspaper or eat?"

Cheryl smiled. "Yeah. I thought I'd catch up on everything. Did you see this?" She tapped the article that she had been reading.

"Young Man Dies after Ten Years as a Quadriplegic," the headline read.

"Yeah," Kathy said. "I remember hearing about that. It was terrible. A buggy had stopped in the middle of the road at night. I think I remember reading that it had some sort of trouble with its wheels. This young man was speeding down the road. They suspected he might have been drinking, but it became a moot point after he was paralyzed. No one else was injured, so I don't think they took it any further."

"What about the buggy that he hit?"

"Nobody was in the buggy, and the man who owned the buggy was outside. The horse thankfully was spared just like the man. The English boy was the only one." Kathy gasped. "You know what? I'd forgotten. Albert Yoder was the man driving the buggy that night."

The news shot through Cheryl like an electric shock. "You don't say."

Kathy eased into the chair opposite Cheryl. "It seems the man can't catch much of a break these days."

"I would hardly say ten years between tragedies is not being able to catch a break." But she supposed any tragedy was more than enough. "So this young man, Greg Smith," Cheryl said, "he was a quadriplegic for ten years?"

Kathy nodded. "He was only like eighteen when it happened. So sad. His parents died right after that if I'm remembering right. That left his sister to take care of him."

Cheryl couldn't imagine and said a quick prayer for everyone involved. How did one get through something like that? Most likely the sister was left to care for the brother. And no doubt there were medical bills stacked up one on top of the other. Hopefully they got some kind of assistance, or the poor girl would probably be paying medical bills until she died. It was a shame. A senseless accident that left utter tragedy in its wake.

"I came to tell you though," Kathy said, "I'll set up box lunches for the auction. Will that help?"

Cheryl smiled and folded the paper back to rights. "That would be wonderful. I thank you. Rebekah and Albert thank you. And Naomi thanks you as well."

Kathy smiled. "It's my pleasure." She glanced up toward the door just over Cheryl's right shoulder. A frown puckered Kathy's brow.

Cheryl half-turned in her seat to see what caused the unusual expression. "What's wrong?"

"Him." She nodded her head toward the man entering the Honey Bee Café.

"Who's him?"

"That's Kip Elliott. Supposedly brought here by the EPA."

Cheryl turned the rest of the way around and watched the man as he sped to the counter. "Does he always walk that fast?"

"Every time I've seen him."

"So what's he doing here?"

"I've heard someone called him about the problem out at the Yoders' farm, but I don't know anything for certain."

"The missing milk?" What did possibly stolen milk have to do with the EPA?

"No, the thing with the manure. Or at least that's the word around town. I'm not even sure what's going on out there."

"It's a bit of a mess," Cheryl said, explaining as best she could what Naomi had told her about the manure problem at the Yoders' farm. "But then they knocked down half of the barn and busted a water pipe. I'm not sure if they will ever get that farm back in order."

"And then this guy." Kathy nodded toward the man placing his order at the counter. "He seems to want to stir things up. That can't be good for Albert Yoder or his family."

"What do you mean?"

She pointed to the man at the counter who took his sack and walked away as fast as he entered. "He came in here two days ago and started quizzing my staff about whether or not the products were organic and if we offered anything vegan. Not vegetarian, mind you, vegan."

Cheryl shook her head. "I guess it takes all kinds. Me? I like chicken too much for that."

Kathy smiled in agreement.

"That makes me think," Cheryl started, "have you been out to the new restaurant?"

"Chicken Pluck?"

Cheryl nodded. "They were so busy. I hope they aren't taking business from the Honey Bee Café."

Kathy shook her head. "Nah. We're doing just fine."

"Have you signed the petition for the legalization of the sale of raw milk in our county?"

"No."

"But do you think it's strange that the two of them came to town at the same time?"

"The restaurant owner and the EPA guy?"

Cheryl nodded. And just when Yoder was having so many problems with his farm. Was there a connection? There was no way to be certain, but it sure seemed like a strange coincidence to her.

Cheryl said her farewell to Kathy then headed back to the Swiss Miss.

She was almost back to her store when she noticed a crowd gathering across the street. The Gleasons' lot had been converted to a fireworks stand for the holiday, but since that had passed, it seemed it was attracting a crowd for an entirely different reason.

"Do you know how bad methane gas is for the environment?"

A few murmurs rose from the spectators. That's when Cheryl realized two things: the man talking was none other than Kip Elliott, and he was speaking into a megaphone.

This was no impromptu gathering.

Cheryl changed directions, nudging her way through the crowd to get to the front of the fray. She supposed that Elliott felt he needed to get his message out and had a ready crowd as the citizens of Sugarcreek prepared for the upcoming Swiss celebration.

"Methane gas is extremely bad for the environment. And where there's a large grouping of cows, there is more methane gas than the area can handle. Good folks of Sugarcreek, it is time to take your village back. Take your clean air back. It's time to get rid of the cows."

Was he serious?

Evidently so. He worked his way through the crowd with a stack of papers. He handed one to anyone who would stop long enough to take it. Cheryl wasn't about to point out to the man that the paper his protest was written on couldn't be that good for the environment, but from what she knew of this guy, it was printed on completely recycled paper with biodegradable and naturally organic ink.

He handed her a flyer as he pushed his way past. Cheryl fisted it in one hand and headed back to the Swiss Miss.

"Whatcha got there?" Lydia asked as Cheryl came in.

Cheryl straightened the paper flat against the Swiss Miss counter and started to read. She had hoped that it would contain some kind of incriminating evidence. Maybe Kip Elliott in all his disdain for cows and their gastric issues was somehow involved with the problems that Albert Yoder was having.

I wonder if anyone else is having any of the same problems with missing milk and malicious pranks.

"Methane gas?" Lydia asked. She wrinkled her nose as she peered over Cheryl's shoulder to read the flyer.

"You know, cow..."

Lydia held up one hand to stop the flow of her words. "Don't say it." She briefly closed her eyes as if she were gathering herself together, then she turned her gaze back to Cheryl. "Does he really think that the Amish people of Sugarcreek are going to give up dairy farming just because he says it's bad?"

"I'm not sure what he thinks, to tell the truth."

"Most of the folks around here have been dairy farming for generations. I don't think they are going to change their livelihood on the word of one man."

She had a point, Cheryl thought as Lydia sashayed away. The young girl grabbed the duster and started back to work before Cheryl could remind her of the afternoon chores.

The Amish wouldn't suddenly convert to this new way of thinking just because one man urged them to. It was the English influence that he was after. And one thing was certain: Kip Elliott had come to town to stir up trouble. But whether or not he had targeted Albert Yoder remained to be seen.

CHAPTER FIVE

Are you sure you're up for this?" Cheryl glanced worriedly at the woman walking between her and Naomi. Rebekah Yoder looked like she could give birth at any minute as she waddled along toward the glass doors of the Sugarcreek Police Department.

Rebekah nodded, though it seemed the closer they got to the doors, the slower her footsteps became.

"You don't have to go in," Naomi said.

Cheryl noticed that the woman had wrapped her fingers around Naomi's arm to steady herself as they walked. Never having been pregnant herself, Cheryl could only imagine how Rebekah felt. With her protruding belly and swollen ankles, the poor woman looked miserable. Add to that the fact that her husband was in jail and she had six little ones at home to take care of, well, it didn't make for an optimal situation.

"Ja, I must."

There was one thing Cheryl could say about the woman: she was tough as nails. She supposed she had to be with everything she faced right now.

The cool interior of the police department building was welcome after the intense July heat. But it seemed to offer no comfort to Rebekah. She stopped still, her eyes wide as she took in her surroundings. Cheryl supposed this was the only time Rebekah had ever seen the inside of the police department.

Then as if by some higher force, she set her feet into motion again, and together the three of them walked to the reception desk.

Delores glanced over her thick-rimmed glasses at them and smacked her gum before asking, "You want to see the chief?"

So Cheryl had come in from time to time to visit with the chief. There was no sense in Delores getting snippy. "Rebekah would like to see her husband."

Delores gave a short nod then indicated that there were vinyl-covered chairs sitting against one white-painted wall. "You can wait there." She picked up the phone, completely dismissing them as she set about to arrange for Rebekah and Albert to see each other.

Cheryl led Naomi and Rebekah to the blue chairs, feeling as if she'd been sent to time-out.

"So we just wait?"

"It shouldn't be long," Cheryl assured her. At least she hoped not. Rebekah looked more miserable by the second. Cheryl knew it was hard on her to come here. She'd left her children at the farm by themselves. Well, not completely by themselves, but Cheryl wasn't sure a sixteen-year-old cousin was wholly sufficient to watch the six Yoder girls while their mom came to town. But that seemed to be a hallmark of being Amish—making do with what you had at the moment. Samantha, sweet and young, was all Rebekah had by way of a babysitter today.

"I hope not," Rebekah said. Her mouth turned down with worry, and instinctively Cheryl reached out and patted one hand reassuringly. She wanted to offer words of comfort but could find none and was saved having to search for them by a uniformed officer who stepped in front of them.

"If you'll follow me."

Cheryl stood and helped Rebekah to her feet. She wanted to go with the woman to support her, but at the same time she knew that Rebekah needed a little time alone with her husband. They would want to discuss things that were no concern of hers. They could keep their conversation in Pennsylvania Dutch, but Cheryl knew face-to-face alone was better by far.

With a worried heart, she watched as the uniformed police officer gently led Rebekah down the hallway toward the visitation rooms.

Cheryl eased back into her seat.

"She doesn't look good." Naomi glanced down the hallway as if somehow her worried thoughts would follow the woman.

"Do you think it's just because she's so miserably pregnant right now?" Cheryl had no idea.

"Ne, there is more to it than that."

"Like what? The baby?"

Naomi gave a small nod. "That baby is coming soon."

That might very well be, but Cheryl prayed that it wasn't right now. Not today. She really wanted an opportunity to try to get Albert out of jail before Baby Yoder decided to make an appearance.

"Should one of us go back there with her?" Cheryl couldn't stop her worrying.

"Ne," Naomi said. "She has got a little time. But not much. We need to get in touch with the midwife soon."

Cheryl nodded. Naomi had had three of her own. She would know more than Cheryl about the timing of babies. As soon as they left, they would get in touch with the midwife and have her on alert that Rebekah was soon to go into labor. Again Cheryl couldn't stop the worry over the woman, her little girls, and the baby on the way. They would need all the help they could get.

Minutes ticked by as they sat side by side in silence. It felt like Rebekah had been back there with Albert forever, but when Cheryl looked, it had only been twenty minutes.

Cheryl wasn't sure how long they would allow her to stay with him, but she knew the woman needed all the time with her husband that she could get.

From across the foyer a phone rang, and Cheryl was vaguely aware of Delores answering it. A few minutes later she pushed back from the desk and made her way to the chief's office. Something in her posture snagged Cheryl's attention, but whatever was said was uttered behind a closed door. Yet Cheryl had a feeling whatever it was, it was important.

Delores came back out, still shaking her dark head, and settled back down behind the reception desk.

Cheryl pushed to her feet.

"Where are you going?" Naomi asked.

"Wait right here." Cheryl made her way over to Delores's desk, mulling over the words as she went. "Has there been any reconsideration on the amount of Albert Yoder's bail?" She figured there hadn't been, but she thought she should ask just in case. The way Rebekah was walking and the pinched slant of her mouth coupled with Naomi's concerns that the baby was coming soon had Cheryl trying to think of different ways to get Albert out of jail. Unfortunately bail was their only solution, so bail it would have to be.

Delores stopped stacking papers and once again surveyed Cheryl over the top of her glasses. "As a matter of fact..."

"As a matter of fact," the chief said from his office doorway, "his bail has just been raised."

From behind her she heard the rustle of cloth and knew that Naomi had jumped to her feet. She might be Amish and not well-versed in all the ways of the English world, but she knew enough to understand that raising Albert's bail was not a good thing.

"Why was it raised?" If anything, she would've thought they would have lowered it. Didn't his standing in the community and the fact that he never had a previous charge count for something?

"Well, it seems there have been a lot of people gettin' sick over this milk deal, and one of them even died."

Naomi gasped.

Cheryl swallowed hard. That was not good news. Not good at all.

"But you don't really know that Albert is guilty," Cheryl said. "Or that whoever stole his milk didn't refrigerate it properly. Maybe they even poisoned it." The words were vapid at best. It wasn't the chief's job to determine innocence or guilt, but to collect the facts. And all the facts seemed to lead to Albert Yoder. Which was ridiculous.

Cheryl was convinced of his innocence, but it was oh so evident that the chief was not. But maybe she had planted a seed and the chief and the other law enforcement officers would investigate this particular angle. She was afraid it might be the only way to prove Albert was innocent. Why would he poison his own milk and then sell it? "Is he going to be charged with murder?" Cheryl asked. That was the last thing they needed. A murder charge would most likely revoke his bail. Then where would they be?

"That'll be up to the judge to decide. They're gonna charge him over there in the next county."

Great. And if they charge him in that county with higher charges, then chances were he would be extradited. And miles and miles away from his family and pregnant wife.

Before Cheryl could protest, Rebekah slowly waddled back down the hallway, her face pale and pinched. Cheryl had been worried that seeing Albert might be too much for her, and the dull light in her eyes was enough to attest to that. The uniformed officer beside her released her arm and stepped back out of the way.

Naomi rushed over, not quite touching but somehow fussing over Rebekah all the same. Then Naomi threaded her arm through Rebekah's and led her toward Cheryl.

Halfway there, the woman stopped. Her hands clutching the bottom of her belly, her lips white with pain.

Before Cheryl could even ask about her condition, the woman's knees hit the floor with a dull thud.

Cheryl raced over as Naomi asked, "Rebekah? Can you stand?"

Rebekah's head was bowed, only the top of her prayer kapp showing. But her whimper was enough to let Cheryl know there was trouble. At least she thought there was trouble. She'd never been around anybody who had gone into labor before, just the things she saw on TV. This was nothing like that. She met Naomi's eyes over the hunched form of Rebekah Yoder.

She didn't even have to ask. Naomi just shook her head slightly then turned her attention back to Rebekah. "Cheryl's here too, Rebekah. We need to get you on your feet and home."

"Midwife," Rebekah managed.

"Hospital," Cheryl countered.

By then the chief had come over, hovering as only a man can do when a woman is in need.

"Rebekah," Naomi started, doing an admirable job of trying to coerce the woman to her feet, "you need to go to the hospital."

Hearing the words from Naomi spurred her into action. She grabbed Cheryl's and Naomi's arms and did her best to get back on her feet.

The chief moved around in front of her, and in no time at all, Rebekah was standing once again, though a strong wind would have knocked her back down.

"See?" she said between clenched teeth. "Just get me home and call the midwi—" She broke off again as another pain hit.

"I'll call an ambulance." The chief moved as if he were about to do just that, but Cheryl stopped him, quietly placing one hand on his forearm.

"Just give us a minute."

Naomi switched to Dutch, excluding the rest of them. That was just fine with Cheryl, for a few minutes later, Rebekah nodded. "I will go to the hospital, but no ambulance."

Naomi looked to Cheryl. She snapped to action. "Give me a minute to get my car."

She practically ran to the cottage and hopped into her trusty blue Ford. Then hurried as quickly as she could back to the police station. She pulled up in front and left the car running as she hustled back to the door. She was halfway there when the chief and Naomi came out, leading Rebekah as quickly as they dared.

Gently, they tucked the woman into the car, and they were off again.

The fifteen-mile trip from the police station to the hospital was nerve-racking at best.

Cheryl glanced into the rearview mirror. Rebekah seemed to be holding her own, but how she was really doing was anybody's guess. Cheryl met Naomi's concerned stare and pushed the gas a little harder.

Lord, please don't let the baby come yet. Forget about having Albert there. Cheryl knew that the baby was coming whether the father was present or not. But she didn't want it born in the backseat of her car.

She didn't know the first thing about having babies. Well, maybe she knew the *first* thing. But that was about it. And she surely didn't want a crash course on the roadside.

Eyes back front, Cheryl breathed a small sigh of relief as they passed a familiar blue-and-white hospital sign. Not much longer now.

From the backseat she could barely make out Rebekah's small sounds of distress as they were mixed in with Naomi's constant stream of Dutch words. Cheryl had no idea what her friend was saying, but her tone was reassuring and low.

Finally, Cheryl pulled into the Emergency Room entrance and parked her car, paying no heed to such formalities as parking spaces. She'd worry about that once they got Rebekah inside.

Chief Twitchell or Delores must have called ahead, for as soon as she stopped the car, an attendant rushed out of the hospital with a wheelchair. In no time at all, Rebekah was inside the building being triaged as Cheryl and Naomi found chairs in the waiting area.

Dear Lord, please take care of Rebekah and her baby, Cheryl prayed.

"There are good doctors here, ja?" Naomi asked.

"The best," Cheryl replied as much for herself as for her friend.

"What happens will be part of *Gott's* plan, but..."

"I know." Cheryl leaned her head back against the wall behind her and closed her eyes. The day was still young, and yet it felt like it should already be dinnertime. Stress, she supposed. "I need to call the store and let them know where I am." Wearily she pushed to her feet.

"I should call home too." Naomi stood as well. "And Rebekah's family. I need to tell Samantha and the girls what happened."

Cheryl had almost forgotten the teen who had come to stay with the Yoder children.

"Rebekah's cousins should know she's here and needs help."

"Her cousins? What about the rest of her family?"

Naomi pressed her lips together. "Rebekah's parents died long ago, and all her siblings moved out west. She only has some cousins here in Ohio. Albert only has his father left. *Dawdy* won't be much help. Nor will her cousins, really. They live too far away to do much about it."

"They could offer some support," Cheryl said.

"Ja."

"You make your calls first, and I'll wait with our chairs."

Naomi nodded and headed across the waiting area toward the courtesy phone hanging on one wall. Cheryl sat down and pulled out her cell.

By the time they both had made their calls, a worried-looking doctor was waiting to talk to them.

"How is she?" Cheryl asked.

"Are you her family?" He looked from one of them to the other.

"Her husband is in jail right now, and her oldest child is a minor. The rest of her family lives about an hour from here. We're good friends of hers." Well, Naomi was her good friend. At least that part was completely true.

"We brought her," Naomi added.

The doctor seemed to mull it over then gave a nod. "We're prepping her for surgery now. The baby's breech and coming fast. We need to get him out of there as quickly as possible."

Cheryl searched his face for signs of more than what he was saying, but his worried frown remained steady.

"Are you planning to remain at the hospital until the surgery is complete?"

Everything was taken care of at the Swiss Miss, and Cheryl felt somehow obligated to wait this out for Rebekah. She could only imagine being in the hospital all by herself, waiting on family and friends to arrive.

"Ja." Naomi stepped forward, taking the decision from Cheryl with the one word. "We'll be here at least until her family arrives."

"Then I suggest you move over to our maternity center." He looked around at the stiff-backed chairs in the waiting area. "I daresay you'll be a little more comfortable over there." And in a second he was gone.

A few minutes later, Cheryl and Naomi settled down into what was euphemistically known as the "family area." Even with overstuffed couches and toys to keep little ones busy while they waited on a younger sibling to be born, a waiting area was a waiting area. But the doctor was right. It was much more comfortable here.

"How long do these things take?" Naomi asked. Cheryl wondered if she knew anyone else who had had a C-section.

"I've no idea. Maybe an hour?"

Naomi leaned her head back and closed her eyes. "I wish Albert were here for her."

"Me too," Cheryl said. It seemed as if the charges against him were stacking higher and higher. But with eyewitnesses saying they saw Albert Yoder selling milk illegally, how could they prove otherwise? If he sold the milk at night, it would be dark and hard to tell. She supposed from a distance one Amish man looked like any other. Black pants, black suspenders, blue shirt, straw hat, and beard. It truly could have been anyone selling that milk.

Cheryl turned toward Naomi. "Do you think Marvin Chupp took Albert's milk and sold it, pretending to be him so that he would get in trouble?"

Naomi's eyes widened. "I know the men have had trouble in the past, but it is not our way." She shook her head as if to add emphasis to her words, but something in her eyes seemed to say otherwise.

"I know you don't want to think ill of him, but it's possible, right?"

Naomi's mouth turned down at the corners. "Ja. It is possible."

And the same could be said for any of the men in Sugarcreek. Just because he had a problem with Albert didn't mean that Marvin would go to such lengths.

Any man. The words raced around her head, trying to find purchase in her rambling thoughts. "Any man," she repeated, hoping that saying the words out loud might give them more clarity. "Any man." It could be Marvin pretending to be Albert, or it could be any man . . .

Cheryl sat up straight in her seat. "Why didn't I think of this before?"

"Think of what?" Naomi asked.

"The man doesn't have to be Amish to pretend to be Albert Yoder illegally selling raw milk. He could be English pretending to be Amish." Excitement zinged through her. "It could even be Justin MacLean."

"Who is that?" Naomi's forehead pinched into a frown.

"The restaurant owner. The man who owns Chicken Pluck. He wanted raw milk to serve in his restaurant."

"If he wanted the raw milk for his business, why would he sell it?"

Cheryl slumped back in her seat. "Good point."

Back to square one.

A nurse in cartoon-printed scrubs appeared at the entrance of the family area. "Looking for the family of Rebekah Yoder."

Naomi pushed to her feet.

The nurse smiled as Cheryl also stood. "Congratulations, it's a boy."

Chapter Six

As promised, Cheryl and Naomi stayed until Rebekah's family came. Cheryl had been expecting a cousin or two, but instead she got Dawdy. With his round paunch and gray beard, he appeared to be the quintessential Amish man of advanced age. Cheryl couldn't help but wonder what comfort he would be to Rebekah. But at least she wouldn't be by herself.

Unfortunately Cheryl and Naomi both had their own obligations they needed to get back to. They said good-bye to Rebekah and the new Baby Boy Yoder and drove back to Sugarcreek. Still no closer to finding Albert a way out of jail or figuring out who was pretending to be him while breaking the law.

"Are you sure you know what you're doing?" Cheryl asked Naomi the next day.

"Of course," Naomi replied.

Yet again they were on their way to Albert Yoder's house. Cheryl had called the hospital that morning to check on Rebekah and the baby. Unfortunately Rebekah's incision appeared irritated, and the doctors were concerned about a possible infection. She wouldn't be allowed to come home until the hospital was certain it would heal fine on its own.

"Well, as long as you know what you're doing. Then I'll just do what you tell me to."

Milking cows. Cheryl had never milked a cow in her life. Much less a cow on a dairy farm with all of the equipment and gadgets that were used these days. The only time she'd even seen a cow milked was with hands and a bucket. Oh, and a stool. This would be a whole new experience for her.

They pulled up to the Yoders' farm. Abigail, the oldest Yoder daughter, ran out to greet them. Followed closely by her five siblings. They surrounded the car before Cheryl could even get out. Though Cheryl couldn't recall each of their names from the whirlwind introductions from the day Albert was arrested, she did remember that the youngest was Grace. Samantha Yoder, the young cousin who had come to help, waved to them from the front porch.

"How is Maam?" Abigail asked, her blue eyes intense with worry. She backed up as Cheryl opened her car door.

"She'll be fine," she said, mentally adding a silent prayer that it would be so.

Despite the fact that it had been days since she had last seen the farm, there didn't appear to be much difference between then and now. The only thing she could see was that water wasn't gushing from the ground any longer. Evidently the broken pipe had been repaired. Still, the ground surrounding the barn was lumpy and muddy. It had been staked off as if to prepare it for concrete, though Cheryl couldn't imagine doing anything with the ground other than let it dry. Would the Yoders' farm ever be back to normal?

"Stop." Abigail Yoder halted her at the door of the barn. "Wear these." She pointed to one corner of the barn where a couple of pairs of well-worn Crocs rested. One pair was blue and the other brown, and both were caked with an unknown brown substance that Cheryl preferred to remain unknown. "It gets muddy out here. I would not want you to ruin your shoes."

Cheryl looked down at her running shoes. They weren't her best pair, but with all the mud and...other things all over the barnyard, Cheryl didn't want to take any chances. She toed off her shoes and slipped her sock-covered feet into the blue pair. At least the inside was clean.

"What's first?" she asked, looking from Abigail to Naomi.

"First, Girlie brings the cows into the pen there. Once we have the feed down on each side, then we'll let them in."

Naomi leaned in close, waving the flies away from her face. "That's Mary Rose," she said, pointing toward the girl who was guiding the cows into the large pen. Once it would have had a roof over it, but since that part of the barn had been knocked down, the sun was still shining on their slick brown backs. She held what looked to be half of a broomstick in one hand, but the cows seemed to know what to do and went along into the space without any extra encouragement from the young Yoder.

"Did Abigail call her Girlie?"

Naomi nodded as she slipped into the brown pair of Crocs. "Most Amish families have a 'girlie.' It is just a nickname."

"It's cute," Cheryl said. With her sparkling blue eyes and impish smile, Mary Rose looked more like a girlie than she did her given name.

Abigail showed Cheryl how to take a scoop of feed and sling it on to the strip of tile on either side of the barn. Toward the center of the space, there were thin metal dividers that reminded Cheryl of the racks grocery stores used to keep the shopping carts in one place in the parking lot. Above each stall a plexiglass holder hung containing a paper with the cow's name and any special instructions.

Cheryl read some of the names and couldn't help but smile. Brownie, Snickerdoodle, and Caramel were among the most delicious-sounding names. There was also a Debbie, Joan, and Amber mixed in with the unlikely name of Brad. Who named a milk cow Brad anyway?

"Are you ready?" Abigail asked.

"As I'll ever be," Cheryl muttered, waving at the flies once again. She didn't know how the cows stood all the pesky insects.

Flies in the buttermilk, shoo, fly, shoo.

Naomi smiled, and Girlie let the cows come into their part of the barn.

Girlie walked beside them, nudging and directing with the stick she held. The gentle reminder kept them from wandering off since the walls to the barn were absent between the actual milking stalls and the holding pen.

So that's why she has that. Cheryl watched as the cows tried to meander off, only to be directed back by a soft prod from Girlie.

For the most part the cows were gentle and obedient, each one entering its stall and waiting patiently for the milking to begin. At her best count, Cheryl figured there were about fifty, though a couple of the stalls were empty.

"Why isn't that one coming in?" Cheryl nodded toward the cow that flopped down in the thick mud.

Abigail shot her a quick smile. "That one is a bull."

"Oh." Cheryl laughed at her blunder and started hooking the collars the cows wore to the chains at the front of each milking stall.

"We're going to feed the horses," Naomi said. Girlie stood just behind her.

"We will pull down the silage first so you won't have to do that if you get done before we're back."

Cheryl tried not to let her confusion show. Her lack of understanding wasn't important. Abigail nodded her agreement, and that was the main thing.

Then Abigail turned a small metal lever, and from somewhere in what was left of the original barn, an air compressor kicked on and the milking began.

Abigail cleaned each cow's teat before attaching the milking apparatus. There were four in all, each clipped to a large metal milk jug. Once one cow was milked, Abigail removed the suction tubes and clipped it on to the extra milk jug, leaving the full jug in the center aisle for Cheryl to dump into a larger jug on wheels.

"That is the sputnik," Abigail explained, bending down to clean the next cow's udder.

"Why's it called that?" Cheryl asked.

Abigail shrugged. They had only been milking a few minutes, but already Abigail's dress was showing signs of dirt and a few wet spots from wringing out the rag she was using on the cows.

Cheryl looked back to the wheeled jug…sputnik. It seemed someone had a sense of humor. "What happens to it when it's full?"

Abigail finished attaching the hoses to the cow's udder and pointed to one end of the barn. A white-painted door stood half open, and Cheryl caught just a glimpse of the shine of a stainless-steel tank inside. "We take it in there and dump it into the main vat."

"And that's where you keep the milk until the truck comes?"

Abigail nodded.

Cheryl wished she could see more of the tank from where she was standing, but she would just have to wait until the sputnik was full. Until then she vowed to find out as much about the milking process and the Yoder milk as she could.

"Why don't you have any black-and-white cows?" Cheryl asked. All the cows were a caramel brown color with sweet faces and big eyes.

"These are Jersey cows," Abigail explained. "They give a richer, creamier milk." She shrugged as if she thought everyone should know that. "Daed only uses Jerseys these days."

Cheryl looked over toward the Chupp farm. The windows on each side of the barn were too high for her to actually see the other farm, but she nodded in its direction regardless. "What about your neighbor? What kind of cows does he have?" She wished she had paid more attention to the cows when they were outside.

"He has a few Jerseys, but I think he will not get a herd because Daed did. You know, he has to compete but in his own way."

"Have they really been at it for a long time?"

Abigail nodded. "As long as I can remember."

Fifteen minutes later, Abigail declared the sputnik full enough to empty. While the suction hoses continued to milk cows, Cheryl and Abigail pushed the wheeled vat into the milk room.

The milk tank was a lot larger than Cheryl had imagined. "How many gallons does this hold?" she asked. And how much of it would have to be gone for someone to notice?

Abigail told her the capacity of the milk tank, but Cheryl was too busy studying the actual tank to fully register the stated size.

"How do you suppose someone could have stolen the milk from here?"

Abigail's head snapped up. She had been monitoring the syphoning of the milk from the sputnik into the tank. "You believe me?"

"Why wouldn't I?"

Abigail shook her head. "Because it sounds ridiculous to even say it."

"But you said you milked the cows and then when the truck came there wasn't enough milk."

"That is right."

"So how would someone steal the milk?"

Abigail's face lit up with happiness that someone believed her fantastic tale. "I have been thinking about that, and the best I can figure, someone brought their own milk jugs or even those big pickle buckets like at the restaurants. Then they filled them up here and took them away." Abigail pointed to door. "They would not have far to tote them. And..."

"If it was dark, then no one would even see them," Cheryl finished.

They were just turning the cows back out into the pasture when Marvin Chupp started across the road. Cheryl had noticed that he had come outside just as she and Naomi pulled up, but she had made no move to greet him. She didn't want him to know that she had noticed. That way she could surreptitiously watch him for suspicious behavior. Unfortunately the milking had to be done in the barn, and she had lost sight of him early on.

"Good afternoon, Marvin Chupp," Naomi greeted. From the sound of her voice, Cheryl figured her friend was about as happy to see him as the eldest Yoder. Samantha crossed her arms, her expression closed and unreadable. Abigail did the same.

"Good afternoon," he replied. "I see you are back."

Naomi gave him a stiff-necked nod. "Ja, it is the only Christian thing to do."

It seemed as if Marvin didn't know how to respond to that. He simply pressed his lips together and looked around as if seeing the farm for the first time. "Such an eyesore. I will be glad when they are done."

Cheryl was certain that everyone involved would be glad when the renovation was complete, but she didn't say as much.

"Maybe then all the strange things will stop," he continued.

"What strange things?" Cheryl asked. She knew Naomi was far too polite to ask. She might make a dig that Chupp wasn't upholding his end of the neighborly Christian stick, but she would never pry.

"Oh, the usual."

The usual strange things?

"Like the protestors?" Cheryl nodded toward the campaign-like signs lining the front of the Yoders' property. Each one had only one word, but when read in order they stated, "Cows are responsible for our declining ozone." There was even one with a picture of a cow with the red circle and line through it. They hadn't been there when they went into the barn for the milking.

Abigail caught sight of the signs, threw up her hands in obvious exasperation, and started pulling them out of the ground.

"That is the third time this week," Bethany Yoder explained. At ten, she was the second oldest Yoder girl.

Cheryl turned her attention away from Abigail and back to Marvin Chupp. His expression changed in an instant, but not before Cheryl caught the smirk.

Really. For all the love and compassion the Amish showed the world and each other, there was definitely some bad blood between the two men. Cheryl wondered why. Or if it was one of those feuds that had been in place so long that no one could remember what started it?

"At least now that Yoder is in jail, I do not get woken up at all hours of the night."

"He would wake you?" Cheryl asked.

"Ja, he would be leaving at different times all night long. Sometimes in his buggy, sometimes in his wagon, and once or twice in a car."

"A car?" Cheryl asked. "Are you certain it wasn't one of the construction workers?"

"At two thirty in the morning?"

She supposed stranger things had happened, but why would a dairy farmer be running around at all hours of the night? It would be extremely hard to stay up all night then get up at four the next morning to milk the cows. Though now the ideas Abigail had about how someone would steal the milk didn't seem all that far-fetched at all.

Abigail and the other girls finished pulling up the signs and deposited them in the barrel the Yoders used for trash. She dusted her hands as if she had just completed a satisfying task.

Samantha gathered the girls and herded them back into the house.

Strange that there were no signs in Chupp's yard.

"I take it you already pulled up the signs from your yard?" It was beyond prying, but Cheryl needed to know.

"There were no signs in my yard."

Because he had been outside when the culprits drove by? Was he a witness to the event?

One thing was clear: either Chupp was responsible or Kip Elliott had something against Yoder.

Cheryl and Naomi watched as Chupp made his way back to his house.

"Do you think he is telling the truth?" Naomi asked as the door closed behind him.

Cheryl shook her head. "I think he's trying to stir up trouble." After all, why would Albert Yoder be driving a car in the middle of the night?

CHAPTER SEVEN

Cheryl slowed her car then turned into the driveway with a large sign that said Chicken Pluck Farm. The name was still a bit of a turnoff, but Justin MacLean hadn't asked her when he chose the name for his farm-to-table restaurant.

"There." Naomi pointed to a sign, a very temporary sign that only said Parking with a large arrow pointing to the right.

Cheryl turned the car into what essentially was a small graveled parking lot. On a good day, it might hold eight cars. But maybe that was all MacLean was worried about having on his farm at one time.

They got out of the car, and Naomi shut her door, turning around and gazing over the farm with a critical gaze. "It doesn't look like I thought it would."

"What did you think it would look like?"

"I do not know, maybe more . . . Amish?"

Cheryl looked around, trying to see the farm from Naomi's point of view. "Well, first of all this is an English farm," Cheryl pointed out.

"True."

It wasn't like a lot of Amish farms went up for sale. Amish families were large, and the land and house were more likely to be handed down rather than sold. Cheryl had a feeling that MacLean would have loved for his farm to look more Amish. But it still had a very homey feel.

The barn was painted a rich red with a traditional hex symbol over the Dutch doors. Contrary to popular belief they weren't all over Amish country, but it did lend a certain amount of charm. The house was painted a soothing cream color with black shutters and colorful flowers all around.

"Do you suppose he's in there?" Cheryl asked Naomi.

"Why would he be?" Naomi looked from the house back to Cheryl.

"Why would he not?" It was a beautiful house. Plenty big enough for a family of five, much less one man.

"Is he married?" Naomi asked. Evidently her thought process had mirrored Cheryl's.

"I don't know. Maybe that's something we can find out."

Maybe he was married, and it was his wife who was trying to gain illegal raw milk.

Cheryl pushed that thought away. She was beginning to get a little loony over this whole ordeal.

"What are we looking for here anyway?" Naomi asked.

Cheryl shrugged. "I don't know really. Just something."

"Something." They started around the car and over toward the large field. Rows and rows of tomatoes were planted there, and Cheryl recognized squash plants, cucumber plants, and a variety of other vegetables that all looked scrumptious.

"Maybe I should plant a garden at the cottage," she commented.

Naomi laughed. "If you want tomatoes, I will give you some."

"Are you implying that I can't grow tomatoes?"

"I said nothing of the sort."

"Greetings and welcome to the Chicken Pluck Farm!" A young man in faded blue jeans and a T-shirt with a large chicken on the front beelined toward them.

Cheryl had been hoping that Justin MacLean would be out here so she could talk to him some more about his petition, but instead it seemed that one of his cronies would have to do.

"We came out to tour the farm," she said.

"Good, good. I'm Daniel Webster."

Was he serious? Greetings from Daniel Webster? Cheryl squashed that thought. His parents' poor naming choice was in no way his fault.

"Are you going to show us around?" Naomi asked.

"I would love nothing more, but this is a come-and-go sort of place. Feel free to wander around. Any place where you're not allowed will be roped off and marked as Authorized Personnel Only. You may pick one vegetable from the garden, but please no more than that. We do have customers we need to feed tonight. The barn is open right now, though the cows are out in the pasture. We just ask that you stay on the concrete and don't get off, as the cows do not pay close attention to where they drop things." He shot them a smile that was as much apologetic as it was humorous.

"Thank you," Cheryl said. He turned to leave, but Cheryl stopped him. "Can I ask one more question?"

He nodded, but she could tell that he needed to get back to whatever work he was supposed to be doing. "Shoot."

"How many cows do you keep here?"

"We only have three at the moment. We keep them around for aesthetic purposes. Until Justin gets the petition through the Ohio state government." Like that was going to happen. But Cheryl didn't say as much.

"And if you don't?" Cheryl asked.

Daniel shrugged. "I don't know. You'll have to ask Justin that."

And that was something that Cheryl would really like to do. "Is he around?" Cheryl asked.

Daniel backed away two steps before answering. "No, he's in town. Enjoy your visit." Then he turned on his heel before Cheryl could ask one more question and hurried off.

"Do you think that's weird?" Cheryl asked Naomi.

"That he practically ran away from you?" Naomi asked in return.

"Yes, and that Justin's not here."

"Where else would he be?"

Cheryl checked her watch. It was one thirty. "The Chicken Pluck is only open for dinner, so he wouldn't be at the restaurant. Maybe in town with his petition?"

Naomi shrugged. "Or running errands."

"Yeah, but if he's going to be a chef and a farmer, don't you think he should be out here more?"

Naomi looked around the farm once again. "It is not a huge farm, and it seems like he has a lot of employees."

"Yeah, I guess you're right," Cheryl said. "But it just seems as if he's everywhere at once."

"And that is a bad thing?"

Cheryl shook her head. "No, but it's strange."

"Ja? He may be in a lot of places, but he is not here."

"You have a point there."

They walked around the grounds, checking into everything they could. Unfortunately, there wasn't a whole lot to it. It was a farm with chickens, dogs, and pigs.

"It's clean, ja?" Naomi said. She half-turned, gesturing with one arm at their surroundings.

Cheryl nodded. She supposed for a farm it was clean, and after witnessing all the trouble the Yoders were having, this farm looked especially neat and orderly. "Maybe because it's new."

"Maybe." Naomi continued to look around as if she couldn't figure out what it was, but there was something wrong with the farm. "There!" She pointed toward the house where a man was standing on the porch. "Is that Justin MacLean there?"

Cheryl squinted at the figure, but couldn't be sure. He dressed like MacLean with ratty jeans, a faded T-shirt, and rope sandals. "I think it is. Let's go talk to him."

"Mr. MacLean," Naomi called as they started across the yard. She had a purpose in her stride, and Cheryl followed in her wake.

The man turned and waited for them to draw nearer before he shaded his eyes. "Hello."

"Your farm is amazing," Naomi said, coming to a stop in the grass below the porch.

"Thank you." If he thought the comment was strange, he didn't say so. "Are you enjoying your visit?"

"It's beautiful," Cheryl said.

"We are doing our best to give our patrons the freshest food possible. We would like to include fresh milk straight from the cow. Please consider signing the petition to legalize the sale of raw milk here in Sugarcreek."

Cheryl frowned at him. "I can't sign your petition. I already told you that."

"Oh yeah. Right." But no recognition lit his eyes. "Thanks anyway. Enjoy your visit." He turned and made his way into the house, leaving Cheryl and Naomi staring after him.

"That was weird," Naomi said.

"Very." Cheryl continued to stare at the green-painted front door as if somehow the answer would just appear. "I guess he sees a lot of people every day."

"Ja, I am sure he does." But Naomi didn't seem convinced.

They headed toward the car, each one lost in her thoughts. They were halfway there when Naomi stopped.

"Wait a minute," she muttered, heading back toward the house.

"Where are you going?" Cheryl started up the small hill after Naomi.

"I thought at the time it was strange. But then after he... It is very strange." She seemed to be lost in her own thoughts, and Cheryl knew better than to try to draw her out of them. Instead she just followed behind her until they reached the second barn on the property. A large green-and-white sign was posted on the door: Authorized Personnel Only.

"What are you doing?" Cheryl asked as Naomi reached for the handles.

"Just looking around." Naomi peered one way and then the other to see if anyone was watching then creaked the door open just a bit. "It spites me that it is so dark in here."

"Here." Cheryl fished around in her purse and got out her cell phone, turning on the flashlight app. She handed it to Naomi who shined it into the dark interior of the barn.

"Look at that!" Naomi pointed inside, and Cheryl peeked around her shoulder to see what she was talking about. Inside the barn two Amish buggies and a wagon waited in the darkness.

"What do you suppose he's doing with those?" Cheryl asked.

Naomi pressed her lips together then pushed the barn door shut. She handed Cheryl her phone then started toward the car once again. "I do not know, but it cannot be good."

In three strides Cheryl caught up with her friend. "You don't think he's using those to go out to the farm and steal Albert's milk, do you?" She didn't want to say the words. It just didn't seem quite right, but what else was an English man doing with two Amish buggies and a wagon?

"But what I do not understand are the buggies," Naomi said. "You can do all sorts of things with a wagon. And it is a farm. He could do hayrides in the fall. That one doesn't concern me. But what is he doing with buggies?"

"I don't know," Cheryl said.

By then they had made it back to the car. Cheryl unlocked it and slid behind the wheel. She sat there for a second, thinking about what they had discovered.

"How did you know the buggies were in there?" she asked Naomi.

"I did not. But why would you have a whole building for authorized personnel only? It just did not make sense to me."

Cheryl nodded and started the car. "So you think it's authorized personnel only because he's trying to hide it?"

"What else could it be?" Naomi asked.

Cheryl mulled it over as she pulled on to the highway and started back toward town. "I don't know. Maybe he . . ." She let her words trail off. "Maybe he likes to ride in buggies."

Naomi shot her a look.

"Because he is crazy English?" Cheryl asked.

"Maybe," Naomi said.

But one thought kept resurfacing time and time again. The man wanted milk, and Albert Yoder had it. Albert lived in the middle of a bunch of other Amish houses. What better way to steal it than with a horse and buggy?

But Cheryl knew that finding the buggy on Justin MacLean's property didn't really mean anything. Not at all.

Going to the Chicken Pluck restaurant for supper—that would be the defining moment. Maybe then she could find out what Justin MacLean was really doing.

CHAPTER EIGHT

Cheryl pulled her car to a stop in front of the Miller house and cut the engine. She was looking forward to the evening and eating supper with Naomi. Not to mention the added bonus of doing some more investigating of the restaurant and its owner.

This afternoon's strange exchange was still ringing through her brain. Something was up with the restaurant owner, but Cheryl wasn't sure how much of it had to do with raw milk and how much of it was something else entirely.

And then there were the buggies and the wagon. Not one but two buggies and a wagon hidden away where no one was supposed to see them. Was it for safety reasons that they were hidden in the barn? Or was it for something entirely more sinister? Whatever the reason, she intended to find out.

She had spent the last two days trying to figure out a way to get Albert out of jail. Between constantly thinking about that and working at the Swiss Miss, Cheryl was looking forward to having a relaxing dinner with her friend. And checking out Justin MacLean just a wee bit more.

The front door opened before she could even knock. "Cheryl Cooper, come in." Elizabeth Miller stepped back to allow her to enter.

"Hi." Stepping into the Miller house was beginning to feel like coming home. The comfortable main room with its polished wood floor, beautifully carved rocking chairs, and a mahogany cabinet filled with various pieces of china and glassware had become as familiar to her as Aunt Mitzi's cottage.

"Cheryl? Is that you?" Naomi came out of the kitchen, her face flushed with heat and her voice harried.

"You don't look ready to go. Did something happen?"

Naomi pressed her lips together then motioned for Cheryl to follow behind her into the kitchen. "One of the Yoder girls called. Samantha's maam fell and hurt her hip so she had to go home." She turned back toward the stove and the number of bubbling pots there. "Now there's no one to help the girls tonight."

Cheryl looked from the stove top to Elizabeth, who merely shrugged. Cheryl had so wanted tonight's dinner to be a treat for her friend, but she couldn't ask why Elizabeth couldn't help so she and Naomi could go to eat. Naomi saw a need and would do everything in her power to fill that need, even if it meant her own plans had to be tossed aside.

"Do you need me to help?" she asked.

Naomi shook her head. "No sense in both of us missing dinner."

"I can't very well go alone." Well, she could. She just didn't *want* to.

Naomi tuned around and snapped her fingers. "I know. Why don't you and Levi go?"

Just then Levi came into the room, his hair damp and dark as if he had just come from the shower.

"Levi," Naomi started, "Cheryl and I were going to eat in town tonight, but now the Albert Yoders need my help. Can you go with her tonight and keep her company?"

He snatched a slice of cucumber off the cutting board and gave his mother a perplexed look. "Ja, sure."

Cheryl looked from one Miller to the other. When she got to Elizabeth, the young girl turned away. But Cheryl couldn't tell if it was on purpose or bad timing on her part. But it seemed as if something was amiss…

"Are you ready to go?" she asked him. He looked ready to go.

"Let me get my hat."

Fifteen minutes later, Cheryl and Levi were in her car and on their way back to town.

She cleared her throat, not quite sure how to broach the subject. "Did you know about this before I got to the house tonight?"

"Know about what?" He turned his attention to her, his eyes curious if not a bit guarded.

"That your mother wasn't going to eat with me tonight."

"She told me when I came in. Then said I should take a shower. So I did."

"But you didn't know that she was going to ask you to come eat with me?" She chanced another look in his direction. They were getting closer to town, and the traffic was picking up. She didn't want to take her eyes off the road for too long, but she wanted to see his face when he answered. Maybe she should have held off asking these questions until they got to the restaurant.

"Ne. You do not mind, do you?"

"No, no," Cheryl assured him. "It's just…"

"You think she did this on purpose?"

She almost laughed as he said the words. "I think maybe she's taking advantage of the situation."

"But why would she want us to go to dinner together?"

Why indeed? "Maybe this is her way of allowing us to get to know each other better without everyone else around."

He gave a sage nod. "That makes sense."

Did it?

Cheryl pulled her car into the packed parking lot of the Chicken Pluck and found a space in the next-to-the-last row of cars. Justin MacLean had definitely found a sweet spot in Sugarcreek. With all the Amish restaurants in the area that served authentic food, Cheryl would have never dreamed that a farm-to-table restaurant would appeal to so many.

She and Levi got out of the car, and Cheryl tamped down the strange feeling of being on a date with him. Not just him. An Amish man. She shook her head. She was getting fanciful in her old age, but she couldn't shake the feeling that she and Levi had been set up. And by his own mother!

The waiter seated them and gave them the paper menu. Levi held it in his big hands as if it were about to catch fire any minute.

"Why are we doing this again?" Levi asked as the server moved away with promises of returning with water and sliced veggies to start.

Cheryl glanced over her menu and caught his steady gaze. He really was a handsome man. She shook the thought away. But, handsome or not, they were from two very different worlds.

"We're looking to see what's on the menu that might include raw milk."

Levi nodded and went back to the menu. "And why do we need to know about this?"

Cheryl leaned in a little closer, ignoring how good he smelled, like detergent and soap. "Did your mother tell you about what happened last week at the Yoder farm?"

"She said that Albert was taken to jail for illegally selling his milk."

"That's right," Cheryl said. "But neither one of us believe that he's guilty. And he's saying that his milk has been missing the last couple of times that the milk truck has come. The owner of this restaurant is circulating a petition to legalize the sale of raw milk."

An understanding light sparked in Levi's blue eyes. "And you think..."

Cheryl nodded but gave a shrug all the same. "It's possible." Anything was possible. But Justin MacLean stealing the raw milk to use in his restaurant was even probable.

Though it didn't explain who was selling the milk.

Their server approached and slid their water glasses in front of them and a plate of raw veggies to one side. Carrots, asparagus, and corn on the cob.

Cheryl suppressed a shudder. Carrots raw, she could do. But asparagus and corn? Maybe concentrating on mostly raw items wasn't such a good idea after all.

It seemed Levi didn't share her reservations. He bowed his head for a quick silent prayer then snatched a stalk of asparagus from the plate.

"Are you ready to order?" the waiter asked. For the first time since they had entered the restaurant, Cheryl noticed that all of the employees were dressed much in the same manner as the greeter. Calling a man dressed in faded blue jeans and a gingham shirt a maître d' was more than she could muster.

Cheryl sent up an apologetic smile. "I'm sorry. I think I'm going to need another minute."

He nodded and tucked his pencil behind one ear. "I'll be back in a few."

"What sounds good?" Levi asked.

"I don't know yet." Cheryl didn't look up from the menu as she studied it. Her mind wasn't on what she might eat, but if any of the recipes might contain milk. Perhaps raw milk. More specifically, raw milk stolen from Albert Yoder.

"I'm thinking about the fried chicken with green beans and new potatoes."

That sounded promising. MacLean would need milk to bread the chicken before frying it to the promised "crunchy, golden brown."

"That might be it." And it came with corn bread. She wasn't much of a cook, but a person needed milk to make corn bread. And butter to serve it with.

Other than that, there didn't seem to be much on the menu that could contain milk. At least not large amounts of it.

"How come I get the feeling that you are not talking about what you're going to eat?"

Cheryl peeled her gaze from the menu and settled it on Levi.

He smiled, and that unwelcomed little zing shot through her. He was so completely wrong for her. Why, oh, why, did she have to be attracted to him? "Have you decided what you want to eat?"

As if by magic, the waiter appeared once again, pencil and order pad at the ready.

"I'll have the fried chicken," Cheryl said.

Levi nodded and handed back to the man the photocopied menu.

Cheryl gave hers one last lingering look then handed it to the man as well.

"Did you find what you were looking for?" Levi asked as the waiter moved away from their table to place their orders.

She shook her head. "Not really. I mean, some of the recipes could use milk, and he has milk listed as one of the drinks, but unless we actually saw what sort of packaging it came in, who's to say where it really came from?"

Just as she said the words, another server moved past them toward a table surrounded by the members of a young and growing family. He had two cartons of milk on the tray he carried, each one obviously intended for the small children seated there.

"Well, he obviously doesn't mind serving 'regular' milk, so maybe he's not our guy." She sat back in her seat.

With her attention no longer caught up in the menu, Cheryl felt the acute awareness that was always present when Levi was around. She ignored it and searched her brain for a safe topic of conversation. One that didn't involve the ins and outs of leaving the Amish, or the English trying to convert.

"I saw the saddest thing in the newspaper the other day," she started, grabbing a carrot before Levi cleared their starter plate.

"Oh ja?"

She took a bite and swallowed before continuing. "It was about a young man who died recently after spending the last ten years in a wheelchair. Actually, it was worse than that. I think they said he was a quadriplegic."

"The Englisch boy that ran into Albert Yoder a while back?"

Cheryl nodded. Of course Levi knew about the accident. He'd been around twenty when it happened. "I guess his sister has had to take care of him all these years," Cheryl said, thinking back on her conversation with Kathy Snyder. If what Kathy said was true, Albert Yoder wasn't punished in any way for his part in the accident. If everything Cheryl had heard so far about the situation was true, then it seemed that the judgment was fair. But one detail kept nagging at her.

"What kind of life can two people have like that?" she asked no one in particular.

Levi shrugged. "Sometimes it is better not to question these things and just accept that what happened was part of Gott's plan."

She had heard the sentiment too many times to count since she had been in Sugarcreek. It was a common thought process among the Amish. Cheryl tried to follow the acceptance as much as she could. It cut down on the need to worry about things out of her control. But there were still times when God's will was a hard pill to swallow.

And then there was the money. How much care did a quadriplegic need? A lot, she was sure. Home nurses and hospital stays. No doubt the young man required constant care. The family's bills had to be astronomical.

Cheryl said a quick prayer for all involved then added a thanks for the meal as the waiter approached with their plates.

"It looks goot, ja?" Levi tucked his napkin into the collar of his shirt and picked up his fork.

Cheryl suppressed a smile and picked up her own silverware. "It does at that."

It more than looked good; it tasted wonderful as well. There was definitely something to be said about all fresh food at a meal. Yet as great as the meal was to eat, Cheryl wasn't any closer to figuring out if Justin MacLean was responsible for the missing milk at the Yoders'.

And speaking of Justin MacLean, they were halfway through their meal when he came strolling in the restaurant through the front door.

Cheryl looked at him closely. Why was he coming in the front door? Wasn't he supposed to be cooking the meals?

She looked down at her plate.

Levi must've noticed her change in demeanor. He looked up and caught her gaze. "What is wrong?"

"That man." She discreetly nodded in Justin's direction. "He's the restaurant owner. He's supposed to be cooking the food."

Levi looked from MacLean to the kitchen door, understanding dawning in his eyes. The man wasn't even moving through the restaurant checking on people's orders; he was simply walking through, then he disappeared into a nearby office.

"I am guessing that's not the kitchen," Levi said.

"It's not. Unless there's a door in there that leads from the office to the kitchen." It was possible, she supposed. But how did he come in the front door if he had been cooking this whole time? It was strange for sure, but they didn't have time to figure it out.

The waiter brought their check. Cheryl and Levi reached for it at the same time. Tingles shot up her arm, but Cheryl couldn't jerk away. Cheryl would have paid if Naomi had been sitting across from her. But even more than that, there was no way she could allow Levi to pay for their meal. That was too much like a date. Way too much.

"Let go, Levi. This is my treat."

He shook his head. "I cannot let you pay."

Cheryl couldn't decide which was worse, the unrelenting light in his eyes or having to continue touching him. "I can't let you pay either. Dutch?" she asked.

Levi frowned. "I do not know what you mean."

She smiled. "We split the bill."

"What does this have to do with the Dutch?"

"I don't know. What do you say?"

"You pay half, and I pay half."

Please, Lord, let him make up his mind soon. "Yes."

"Fine," he said. "Ja, this time we are Dutch. But next time we go out, I get to pay."

CHAPTER NINE

C heryl?"

The next afternoon Cheryl answered the phone at the Swiss Miss to hear Abigail Yoder on the other end of the line. "Hi, Abigail. How are you today?"

"I did not know who to call," Abigail said, her voice rising with emotion.

Cheryl glanced around at the few customers milling through her shop. It was three o'clock, and foot traffic was definitely at a low inside the Swiss Miss. Lydia was helping a lady with some quilted goods, and Esther was due in any minute.

Cheryl caught Lydia's gaze and pointed toward her office.

The young girl gave a nod of understanding, and Cheryl ducked inside to finish her conversation in private.

"What's wrong?" she asked Abigail.

"That man is here again. The one who keeps putting the signs in the yard."

"He put signs in the yard today again?"

"No, he's marching up and down the street with a big sign that says something about the ozone and how bad cows are. Are cows really that bad?"

"Calm down, Abigail," Cheryl soothed. "Is he alone?"

"Some people came with him, and more seem to be arriving. I don't understand. Why is he doing this to us?"

"I don't know, honey. Just give me a minute, and I'll be right there."

"Okay," Abigail said, her relief evident. "Thank you, Cheryl Cooper."

Cheryl hung up, grabbed her keys and purse, and headed for the door. She stopped only long enough to tell Lydia she would be back as soon as possible.

The worst part about not driving to work was having to go back and get her car at the cottage in order to drive someplace, but it was a short walk. On the way out the door she passed Justin MacLean. This time he'd taken up on her side of the street where the fireworks stand had been. It was usually the favored place of Kip Elliott.

Oh, how she wanted to go over and ask him about his strange appearance at the restaurant last night. How could he be in two places at one time? He couldn't be. Which meant that someone else had been cooking their food. And what about earlier in the day when she and Naomi were at the farm? She hadn't thought much about it at the time, but Daniel had said that Justin was in town. Then the next thing they knew he was on the porch. Had he just arrived? Or had he been in the house the whole time? And why did it even matter? It wasn't like that was a crime. Or that it had anything to do with the milk disappearing.

No, but it gave her something to think about. Somehow this all tied together. She just couldn't figure out how. For now she had to get over to the Yoders' as quickly as possible.

Cheryl could only hope that the panic in Abigail's voice was an overreaction to the events, but she had a feeling it wasn't.

Why was everybody targeting the Yoders? Or maybe it just felt that way. If Kip Elliott was marching down the road as Abigail said, perhaps he was picketing both farms at one time, the Yoders' and the Chupps'. But Cheryl wouldn't know until she got out there.

She hopped into her car and grabbed her cell phone, dialing Naomi's number and leaving a quick message as she headed down the street. She would have preferred to run by and pick up Naomi on the way, but Cheryl felt like she needed to get to the Yoders' as soon as possible. With Samantha Yoder gone to take care of her own mother, Rebekah in the hospital, and Albert still in jail, Abigail was far too young to have to worry about picketers on top of everything else.

Cheryl drove as quickly as she could to the Yoder farm, pulling up just as the police chief did as well. He gave her a look, its intent undetermined as she shut her car door and approached. "Chief Twitchell."

He nodded. "Ms. Cooper."

"Are you going to allow this?"

Just as Abigail had said, Kip Elliott from the EPA was marching up and down the road with a large sign in his hands. Save Our Ozone, Down with Cows! it read. Elliott had braced it against one hip as he shouted into a megaphone the same words he had painted on his sign. Only a handful of people carried signs and marched behind him with as much intent as an army going to war. Just as Abigail had described, gawkers and sympathizers alike were standing around looking on as if something was about to happen at any minute and they didn't want to miss a second of it.

"Well now, Ms. Cooper, he's on public property."

Indeed he was. Kip Elliott had stayed just to the left of the right-of-way and remained in the road, completely off Yoder property. But why was he facing the Yoder farm instead of the Chupp farm?

As far as Cheryl could tell, there were just as many cows across the road as there were on this side. What made Yoder cows so much worse for the environment than the Chupp cows? Or was Chupp behind it all?

"He's upsetting the girls," Cheryl said. "I'm sure I don't have to remind you that their father is in jail and their mother is still in the hospital. He shouldn't be taking advantage of the young this way."

The chief adjusted his gun belt once again. "I understand. But this is still a free country."

Cheryl was gearing up for a pithy retort when Naomi pulled her buggy into the drive. The woman might be small in stature, but she was big in other ways. She slid from her carriage and came to stand next to the chief. "I suppose there is nothing you can do." Somehow the words were accusing as much as they were explanatory.

"Ms. Miller, unfortunately he's not hurtin' anything, and I can't very well make him leave. It's a peaceful protest."

Naomi gave the chief a nod then started toward the house. All six of the Yoder girls were standing on the porch, watching as the crowd outside their farm grew. "Come on now. Let us go inside," Naomi said, herding them into the house once more. She disappeared behind them, and Cheryl wondered if she were giving them some sort of pep talk along the way.

She had called the hospital that very morning, and with any luck Rebekah Yoder would be discharged by tomorrow afternoon. Of course, it didn't do anything about the protesters who were marching now.

Cheryl swung her gaze over to the barn. As long as it didn't rain, the ground might even be dry enough tomorrow to start laying the concrete. Not that she knew a lot about such things, but it did appear drier than it had the day before. Soon, hopefully, they would have the walls back up and things around the Yoder farm just might return to normal. Just might.

The chief tipped his hat at Cheryl and started back toward his car.

She followed behind him. "You're not leaving, are you?"

Apparently he was. He reached for the handle and opened the door, standing in the V that it made with the body of the car as he waited for Cheryl to catch up to him. "There's no crime here, Ms. Cooper. I need to be where there's actual trouble. You understand."

Cheryl nodded then glanced back toward the protesters. Marvin Chupp was on his front porch, feet up on the rail and a glass of what appeared to be lemonade in one hand. He lifted it in salute then laughed heartily before taking a drink. If she didn't know better, she would suspect that he himself had called Kip Elliott to come out and protest at the Yoder farm. Come to think of it, she didn't know better. But what would Marvin Chupp gain by having such chaos between the two houses? All he was doing at this point was upsetting the girls. Their mother wasn't there. Their father wasn't there. Anybody that he would really want to get even with was gone. Or maybe the feud went so deep that he was happy to upset any of the Yoders, no matter how young.

"I would prefer if you stayed, just in case it turns ugly."

The chief got into his car and started the engine, rolling down the window before replying to Cheryl. "These guys want to save the ozone by gettin' rid of cows in captivity. I doubt they're going to do much by the way of physical harm to anyone around."

"You never know," Cheryl said. Even to her own ears the words sounded ludicrous. "Sometimes it's those docile ones that are the most dangerous."

The chief glanced back over to Kip Elliott with his large sign and megaphone. On the danger scale of one to ten, he rated about a two, and she could see the same assessment as plain as day on the chief's face.

"On that matter, I think we're just goin' to have to take our chances." He shifted his car into gear and backed out of the driveway, careful not to run over any of the peaceful protesters on his way off the farm.

⁓⟨❀⟩⁓

"Are you going to tell me how last night went?" Naomi asked.

Cheryl met her friend's gaze and resisted the urge to shrug. "I think now isn't a good time to discuss that."

The chief was gone, the protesters were still in the road out front, and the girls were locked inside their own house. Last thing Cheryl wanted to do was talk to Naomi about her dinner with Levi. Of course that had more to do with the fact that she didn't understand her dinner with Levi and still hadn't figured it out for herself. There was no way she was telling Naomi that.

"Did you have a good time?" Naomi asked.

Cheryl nodded. "We had a great time. Food was good. The atmosphere was interesting. But we still didn't find out anything about the raw milk petition." Best keep things on track. The dinner had been to discover more about Justin MacLean and his petition to get raw milk legalized in Ohio. Not that Cheryl thought that would be a possibility. But if Justin MacLean wanted raw milk badly enough...

He would have access to quite a few large food containers since he worked in the restaurant industry. Was he the one keeping Marvin Chupp awake? Or was Marvin just making up stories in order to incriminate his neighbor? Too many questions, not enough answers.

"We had a good time." Cheryl sent her friend a small smile. Let her figure out what that meant. Cheryl still wasn't convinced that Naomi hadn't set up her and Levi to go out on this dinner. Yet the longer she studied the idea, the more ludicrous it seemed. Naomi knew just as well as anyone that the relationship between Cheryl and Levi was next to impossible.

Despite the thrills Cheryl got whenever she was in Levi's presence, nothing more could grow between them. Too many differences stood in their way. And that was best something she remember every time he was near. Maybe she should embroider it on a throw pillow. That way she could look at it daily.

"What can we do about the girls?" Cheryl nodded toward the house.

Naomi sighed. "I'm going to stay until I can get a hold of one of the cousins. If these people are going to keep coming out here bothering them, I think they need an adult on the property. With any luck, Rebekah will be home tomorrow. If we can get someone to stay here one night, that would be good, ja?"

"Sure," Cheryl said.

"If not, then I can stay myself. It's only one night."

"And the milking?"

Naomi propped her hands on her hips and gazed up at the sky as if from the sun alone she could tell what time it was. "We have a little bit of time. Maybe the protesters will go home by then."

The loud bark of an air horn drowned out the chants of the protesters.

Cheryl whirled around to see the large milk truck easing down the road. The driver blew his horn again, and the protesters scattered, most jumping down into the shallow ditch between the Yoder farm and the road.

"What in the world...?" Cheryl's question trailed off.

"That would be the milk truck," Naomi said. The driver had pulled up a little farther down the road, then the shrill beep, beep, beep of the backup alert rent the air as he backed his truck into Marvin Chupp's drive.

"Does that mean he'll pick up the milk from here too?" Cheryl asked.

Naomi shrugged. "I suppose so. I don't know for a fact, but I imagine they have the same buyer. Most people around these parts sell their milk to one company that distributes it throughout."

Just then Girlie walked up. "We test the milk each time to make sure there's no contamination before we pump it into the truck."

"But if he gets Chupp's milk in the truck and then comes over here and gets this milk, then it would mix together, right?"

"Oh ja," Naomi said.

"Then why all the concern about the Jersey cows versus the other cows and the creamier milk and all that?"

Girlie shrugged. "A different guy comes here. Daed sells the milk to a special dairy."

Naomi shot her a small smile. "Well, now that explains that."

Maybe all the competition between Marvin and Albert was just two old men bickering over nothing.

Half an hour later, the driver from the dairy that purchased Yoder's milk waited to back his rig into the drive.

The girls came out of the house and laid boards down over the mud that currently served as their driveway.

The driver expertly backed up the truck toward the end of the barn where the milk room was. He got out of the cab and adjusted his baseball cap as he hit the ground.

Abigail met him halfway to the barn door, giving him a nod of greeting.

"Hi there, Miss Abigail," the driver said. "How's your mom?"

Abigail smiled. "They say she may be able to come home tomorrow."

The driver nodded. "And your dad?"

Cheryl almost cried at the dark cloud that floated over Abigail's normally sunny expression. "I do not know."

"That's too bad." The driver went around the truck and pulled out the hose.

Cheryl watched as he dragged it through the door into the milk room. He hooked it up and started a pump that would pull the milk from the large stainless-steel vat into the tanker on the back of his rig. In no time at all it seemed, the milk had been collected.

Abigail shook her head. "That cannot be."

"Is that all?" Cheryl asked. She had just been in the farm the day before. Abigail had shown her the milk that was in the vat. It was almost full when they had finished yesterday's evening milking. Add in this morning's collection, and it should be almost to the top. Surely it would take longer than a few seconds to pump all those many gallons of milk from the tank into the truck. The first driver had been at Chupp's farm a lot longer than this one had been at the Yoders', that was for sure.

The driver looked at the gauges then glanced back to Abigail. "I'm sorry. It seems that's all there is."

For a moment Cheryl thought that Abigail might burst into tears. But she was Amish and not prone to fits of hysterics or drama. Instead of breaking down, the young girl straightened her shoulders and marched into the milk room.

Cheryl heard the scrape of the door as she opened the milk vat then the hollow slam as the lid fell back into place.

Abigail marched back outside. "It is empty," she said. Her voice trembled, though she held her chin at a stubborn angle. "There was much more milk than that yesterday."

Cheryl took a step forward. "There was. I saw it myself." If she thought her words were going to be a relief to Abigail, she was wrong. Then again, knowing that the milk was there and having it gone was not a comfort in the least. Where had the milk gone? That was what they needed to find out.

"Did anybody see anything last night?" Cheryl looked all around at the faces of the young Yoder girls. All of them shook their head.

"Nobody heard anything?"

Again everyone shook their heads. How could somebody come in during the middle of the night, steal gallons upon gallons of milk, and not make a peep?

Or did they? Cheryl turned on her heel and picked her way across the muddy yard, wishing all the while she had the boots that she had worn yesterday to milk. They would have been a far sight better than her black leather flats she had worn to work today.

She checked both ways and crossed over to Chupp's house. The old man was still on the front porch, intently watching everything that happened across the road from him. "Mr. Chupp," Cheryl started. "A word please?" She stopped in the middle of his yard and waited for him to give a nod of consent and come down the porch steps to join her.

The best thing about the milk truck coming, aside from knowing for a fact that the milk had been stolen, was that its presence seemed to scatter the protesters and gawkers alike. Now Cheryl could talk to the man without having to compete with Kip Elliott's bullhorn.

"Ja?"

"You told me a bit ago that there were some things going on over at the Yoder place. Did you hear anything last night?"

Marvin tucked his fingers into the waistband of his broadfall pants and rocked back on his heels as he stared at the sky.

Cheryl resisted the urge to look up and see if the answer was written there and instead took a minute to look back at the Yoder farm and the disaster that still reigned.

"I do not recall."

"You don't recall talking to me? Or you don't recall if there were any problems last night?"

"I cannot rightly say that anything unusual went on over there last night. I slept like a baby all night."

I bet you did. Cheryl looked back at the Yoder farm. Naomi was standing watch as Abigail signed the invoice for the milk. The driver swung back into the cab of his truck. Even from this distance Cheryl could see that the young girl was despondent over the stolen milk.

What if the driver... She pushed that thought away. The driver had all the means to steal the milk. He had a truck and he knew the farm, but why would he only target the Yoders and no other dairy farmers in the area?

"Come to think of it..."

Cheryl swung her attention back to Marvin. "Yes?"

"It seems there was a ruckus last night late. The dogs all started barking."

"Did you hear anything else?" Cheryl asked. "A car? A truck? Maybe a wagon?" Anything. *Just give me anything and let me know if someone was at the farm while Albert Yoder was in jail. That's all I need to take to the chief and get him out of jail.* Well, hopefully. If Albert was in jail, he couldn't be the one stealing milk in the middle of the night.

"I don't remember hearing a truck. Or car."

"A wagon?" A pulley cart, anything.

Chupp shook his head. "I just cannot be certain."

Cheryl resisted the urge to ask him if he truly wasn't certain or if he didn't want to be certain. He was gaining too much joy out of the fact that his neighbor was in jail.

She had to do something. Amish or not, the girls were too young to remain there by themselves for much longer. Even when Rebekah came home from the hospital, she wouldn't be strong enough to carry on with her work as normal, much less having a newborn to care for.

Cheryl remembered that Naomi had explained that Amish women focused mostly on their newborn for six weeks after the baby was born. That meant the girls would be pulling extra duty until their father returned home. Yep, Albert Yoder needed to get home and as soon as possible.

"Thank you anyway." She reached out a hand to shake.

The man stared at it for a couple of seconds before finally deciding to accept.

Marvin Chupp wasn't all bad. She could see that. Now if she could get either one of them to forget their feud, maybe they could figure out who was doing this. Unless that person was Marvin himself.

Cheryl pushed her way into the police station. She was becoming all too familiar with the sights, sounds, and smells of the place.

Delores looked up from her typing and gave Cheryl a quick smile. "Cheryl! How nice to see you."

"Is the chief available?"

"I'll see." Delores turned toward the intercom button, but before she could do anything, the chief called out from his office.

"Come on in, Ms. Cooper."

Cheryl smoothed her hands down over her slacks and made her way inside the office. She had come here straight from the Yoder farm, stopping only long enough to rinse the mud from her shoes before barging in.

"Chief, I need you to let Albert Yoder out of jail."

The chief had been sitting with his feet propped up on his desk, lounging back as if waiting on her to come and make her demands. He dropped his boots to the floor, his chair squeaking with the motion. "Do you now?"

Cheryl propped her hands on her hips and gave him a confident nod. "That's right. I just came from the Yoders' farm, and their milk was stolen last night."

"That's quite an accusation."

"I was there yesterday. I saw how much milk was in the tank, and then I saw how much milk the driver got today. Someone stole their milk in the night. Now, as far as I can see, Albert Yoder was in jail, and he wasn't selling milk illegally. That means somebody is stealing his milk and selling it while pretending to be him so that you'll keep him in jail." She paused to suck in a deep breath.

To the chief's credit, he didn't bust out laughing. Though her accusation sounded so much more put together and sane when it was inside her own head.

"Let me get this straight. You're tellin' me that somebody is stealing Albert Yoder's milk in the middle of the night then pretending to be him and selling it to unsuspectin' buyers?"

"No," Cheryl started, her voice losing some of its urgency. "I think people know that they're buying raw milk. At least some of them probably do, but I don't think they're buying it from Albert Yoder."

"You know I have witnesses."

"You have witnesses that say that a man going by the name of Albert Yoder is selling raw milk. But you don't know for a fact that it's Albert Yoder." Again the sentence sounded so much saner in her head.

"Ms. Cooper." The chief stood, his thin frame urging her toward the office doorway. "I appreciate the fact that you have come into our community and taken such an interest in all the happenings. But I have to say that this is one of those times when you are far from the mark. I understand that you're tryin' to help the Yoders, but I think it's time you just went on home and let me do the investigating."

Cheryl staggered at his condescending tone then managed to regain her footing and eased toward the door. "So you think Albert is guilty and you have the right man in jail?"

"That's right. I've got witnesses, I've got milk, and I've got evidence. I don't need anything else to hold him on those charges. Unless you've come with bail money, I think you should go back to the Swiss Miss and sell some jelly."

Cheryl bit back a growl of frustration. She was going to have to find even more evidence of Albert Yoder's innocence before the chief would believe her. She had known it was a long shot, but she'd had to try. "Those girls need their father at home."

"Most girls do," the chief said. "I understand, and I feel for them. But the fact remains that I must uphold the law, and Albert

Yoder seems to have broken it. There's nothin' more to it than that, Ms. Cooper."

Cheryl turned on her heel and started out of the office.

Delores was back to her typing, though she was going at it a little too furiously for Cheryl to believe she'd been doing anything but listening in on their conversation.

Unable to just walk out, just like that, Cheryl stopped. She wanted to turn around and ask Delores if she believed her theories on who was selling raw milk in Tuscarawas County, but what Delores believed didn't matter. In fact, really what the chief believed didn't matter. Cheryl needed evidence. Hard evidence.

Her gaze fell to the coffee table in the small waiting area. An open newspaper lay on top of the stack of magazines, the pages folded back to an interior article.

"Funeral services held."

There was no reason for the headline to capture her attention, but it did. She picked up the paper, only vaguely aware that behind her Delores had stopped typing.

Cheryl scanned the article. It was another piece about the quadriplegic English boy who had recently died. Cheryl looked over the words, searching for the reason behind it. But she could find none. No politicians or bigwigs came to the funeral. In fact, it seemed as if hardly anyone attended. And that was the tragedy of it all. A young man's life cut short, only his sister left to care for him, and almost no friends left to attend the funeral.

How tragic that in an instant a vibrant life could be reduced to nothing. It was beyond sad.

Cheryl turned toward Delores. "Can I have this?"

Delores shrugged. "Sure. I don't care. It's yesterday's paper anyway."

Cheryl had looked through yesterday's paper, yet for some reason that article hadn't stood out to her then. Today it captured her attention like a magnet pulling metal filings.

She wasn't sure why she wanted to keep the article. She just did. Something about the situation nagged at her, pulled at her thoughts and her heart and made her want to investigate further.

"Thanks." She tucked the paper under her arm and headed for the door.

CHAPTER TEN

After leaving the police station, Cheryl swung back by the Swiss Miss, grabbed Beau and his carrier, then headed home. The article in the newspaper still nagged at her like a toothache.

She let herself into the cottage, wondering if just saying a prayer for the young girl who had lost everything would be enough to take her mind off of it, but as her dinner heated in the microwave, she knew it was more than that.

She grabbed her laptop and sat at the kitchen table, punching the name Greg Smith into the search engine. Article after article came up on different Web sites for different reasons. Charges and hospital stays came up along with images of him in a hospital bed and the car he was driving. Then there was the face of the young woman with straight blonde hair and sparkling green eyes. She clicked on the picture.

April Smith.

The sister of the boy who had been reduced to a crumpled shell during the unfortunate accident.

But Cheryl had seen that face before. Maybe not quite as young and unlined, maybe not as carefree or with eyes that sparkled with such vibrancy. She had still seen that face. She had seen it in the crowd at the Yoder farm.

But why?

Why would a girl who just buried her brother be at a protest over cows? It just didn't make sense. If Cheryl was right about the care that her brother needed, why would April Smith be out protesting anything other than perhaps equal rights for handicapped people?

Cheryl shook her head. She had to be mistaken. But that face and its familiarity badgered her. She just wished she'd been paying a little more attention this afternoon when she scanned the crowd. But how was she supposed to know that tonight she would've thought she saw the girl?

She pushed back a chair and grabbed supper out of the microwave, using two fingers to keep from burning herself against the heated plastic of the serving tray. "I really need to learn to cook," she told Beau.

The kitty gave her a baleful look in return. He blinked his blue eyes then stretched as if he had nothing better to do. She supposed he didn't. But she did. She had to find a way to get Albert Yoder out of jail. And not to worry about why a young girl whose brother had just died was picketing at his farm.

Cheryl turned at the sound of the knock and motioned for her friend to come inside.

"Good morning," Naomi said. She pulled her blue wagon behind her, though it wasn't stacked as high as usual. It had only been a couple of days since Naomi had brought in supplies to restock her products at the Swiss Miss. Cheryl could only assume that she had other business on her mind as well.

"Have you been to the Yoders'?"

"I did. I went down this morning after the milking." She pressed her lips together and shook her head. "Four of the cows are not giving milk."

Cheryl frowned. "I know that's a bad thing, but what happened?"

"I do not know myself. Seth had never farmed dairy cows. But I would suspect maybe hormone shots could do that."

Hormone shots? "Why would someone give a cow hormone shots?" The thought was ridiculous at best, but Cheryl couldn't rule it out entirely.

"The worst of the matter is that they were the four best milk-giving cows they had." Cheryl remembered Abigail's constant stream of information about the milk cows as they conducted the milking the other day. Yet as chatty as the young girl had been, nothing had been said about what caused a milk cow to suddenly quit giving. Cheryl would have to Google it later and see what she could figure out.

"Are you going out there today?"

"That was one of the things I wanted to talk to you about," Naomi said. "One of the cousins is with the girls now, and Rebekah is supposed to get out of the hospital later."

Cheryl nodded. With any luck the Yoder farm would be a couple of steps closer to normal by this afternoon.

"Do you think you could give Rebekah a ride out to her farm?" Naomi asked. "I could hire her a driver, but I have a feeling she would be more comfortable with you. I mean, she will have the new baby and all."

"Of course," Cheryl replied without giving it a second thought. In the last few days the Yoders had come to mean so much to her that she would do just about anything to help them out. Including collecting the donations for the benefit auction that was to be held tomorrow.

"Thank you, Cheryl." Naomi smiled.

"It's the least I could do," Cheryl murmured, saying a little prayer that the benefit auction would go off without a hitch and they would make enough to post Albert Yoder's bail.

*   *   *

After Naomi left, the store officially opened and Cheryl got down to work. There was enough traffic in the Swiss Miss that she didn't have too much time to think about Albert and Rebekah and bail money. Instead she funneled all of her attention into taking care of the customers as they came in and making sure they found the perfect treasure to take back with them to their homes.

"I mean, he wouldn't take no for an answer," a woman in a red T-shirt and an I Love Ohio visor said sometime after lunch.

Her friend nodded. "I told him I didn't live in Ohio, but he just wanted to talk."

"And about milk cows." The lady in the visor shook her head. "I wonder why it means so much to him?"

Her friend shrugged. "He was telling me, but I was more interested in getting away than I was listening to what he had to say." She pressed her lips together and shook her head. "Some people."

Some people indeed.

Cheryl excused herself from the customer she was helping and made her way to the front door. She peeked out just as Justin MacLean approached a lady who was obviously on her way into the Swiss Miss.

MacLean held out his clipboard toward the woman who shook her head and raised her hands as if to stave off anything else he might reply back with.

She took two steps toward the door of the Swiss Miss with MacLean close behind.

The woman shook her head and adjusted the shoulder strap of her purse. She glanced from the clipboard to the shop as if judging the distance between the two and calculating if she could make a quick enough getaway without Justin MacLean noticing.

This has got to stop.

Cheryl held open the door for the lady. The movement must've caught the customer's gaze. She smiled gratefully and ducked inside.

Cheryl returned the smile. "Welcome to the Swiss Miss. Come on in."

Once the lady was safely inside, Cheryl closed the door behind her and crossed the sidewalk toward the restaurant owner.

"I understand that that petition is important to you and your business, but you can't ask for signatures out here."

"It's a free country."

"That may be true, but when you start harassing my customers, their rights have been compromised. Do not bother my customers." She hated getting nasty with the man, but she didn't need customers sidestepping her store just to avoid a determined man who wanted to serve raw milk in his restaurant.

"This is about more than just milk. It's about our freedoms. What else is the government going to take away? You have to wear your seat belt. You have to get insurance. You can't drink raw milk. It's just going to keep going until we have no control over our own lives. We can't let the government dictate every part of our very being. We are sentient beings and should be able to make our own decisions."

He had a point. She supposed if people wanted to drink raw milk and risk the contamination and disease that was reportedly associated with it, who was the government to say that they couldn't?

"That may very well be, Mr. MacLean, and you are more than welcome to circulate your petition. Just not in front of my store. Most of my customers are tourists and are not registered voters in this county."

MacLean made a face.

"I'm sure you understand my position; I'm just looking out for my clients."

MacLean nodded. "Can I leave one in the store for people to read and sign?"

Cheryl shook her head. "I'm sorry, but I don't think that's a good idea. You can see if Kathy Snyder will let you hang up a copy on the Honey Bee Café bulletin board, but I can't make any promises." She made a mental note to apologize to Kathy for dragging her into this mess.

MacLean shook his head. "She said I couldn't leave one there either. Why is everybody so against raw milk?"

"I'm not sure," Cheryl said. And she wasn't. Other than the fact that it *could* carry diseases, what was the harm in drinking raw milk? "I'm sorry, Justin. You'll have to circulate your petition someplace else."

He cupped his hand into his back pocket and gave her a quick nod. "I heard you came out to the farm and took the tour. What did you think?"

Cheryl frowned. "You were there." She studied his face for any type of shock or surprise, but he had his features schooled into a careful mask of indifference.

"Of course." He chuckled. "That's what I meant to say. Did you have a good time?"

"It was very nice. Very clean," she said the words knowing that they sounded a little bit on the downside but she had to say something to keep herself from asking him about the buggies and the wagon she found in the barn. The only way she could tell him that she found them was that she had entered an authorized area. Still, she would've liked to know why he had them.

"Did you enjoy your meal?"

Cheryl turned toward the entrance of the Swiss Miss then stopped. "It was lovely, thank you."

"There's nothing like fresh food. Nothing at all. Now you understand why it's so important that I have fresh milk, fresh butter, and other fresh dairy items to serve in the restaurant. Surely you can understand that."

"I can," Cheryl said. "But I'm also a law-abiding citizen. Good day to you, Mr. MacLean."

She hurried back into the shop. As soon as she got back inside the Swiss Miss, she turned and saw Justin walk down the sidewalk, clipboard tucked under one arm. He might have different views on the government and a host of other things, but it seemed he was nothing if not law-abiding.

How easy would it be if he were the culprit stealing the milk to serve in his restaurant, pretending to have everybody sign a petition so that they would be able to have the milk? But she'd asked him nicely to move on, and he had done so without much of an argument. She couldn't find a lot of fault with that.

Even if she didn't know why he had two Amish buggies in his barn. Or how he managed to be everywhere at once.

The hospital called at three, and the nurse explained that Rebekah Yoder was all packed and she and Baby Yoder were ready to go home. Cheryl wasn't sure exactly how they were going to get the baby home, seeing as how she didn't have a car seat. As far as she knew, neither did Rebekah. She told the girls where she was going, grabbed her purse and her keys, then headed over to the hospital.

Thankfully one of Rebekah's cousins had brought a car seat for her to use with Baby Yoder. It looked as if it had seen a few better days. Cheryl knew the Amish made use of what they had, and this was what they had. Funny how English moms would have to have a brand-new car seat with all the bells and whistles. The most fancy, beautiful, and clean to take the baby home. This one looked clean but faded, sturdy but well-worn. And when Rebekah tucked Baby Yoder inside, he looked just as content as if she had placed him in a golden throne.

Fifteen minutes later the baby was strapped in the backseat, and Rebekah was sitting beside him as Cheryl drove them out to the Yoder farm.

"The girls have missed you," Cheryl said.

Rebekah nodded. "I have missed them too. Naomi's been trying to keep me updated on everything that is going on." She pressed her lips together, and Cheryl wondered if the stress of it all was beginning to get to her. She could only imagine what it felt like to have a brand-new baby, a torn-up farm, her husband in jail, and cow's milk disappearing left and right.

"Did she tell you about the benefit auction on Saturday?"

This time Rebekah's eyes did fill with tears. A couple slid down her cheeks. She used the back of one hand to wipe them away. Then she shot Cheryl a grateful smile. "She did, and it means more to me than you will ever know the help that you are giving us, Cheryl Cooper."

The look on her face squeezed Cheryl's heart. She was only doing what anyone would do in this situation—help out a neighbor and friend. But she knew that so many times people didn't help. Christians walked by strangers who needed a hand up, too busy with their own lives to assist their fellow man.

"It's a blessing to me," Cheryl said. "To be able to help you this way is a true and honored blessing. And I thank you for the opportunity. We've just got to get Albert home."

"Amen," Rebekah said.

Cheryl turned on to the country road that would take them past the Miller farm and over to the Yoders'. "I hate to bring this up, but I think you should know before we get to your house. Some of the cows have stopped giving milk. Is this normal?"

"Cows go dry from time to time. There is nothing we can do about that."

Cheryl shook her head. "Four cows at a time. And the most milk-giving cows in your herd? It just seems strange to me."

Rebekah twisted her mouth into a grimace, and Cheryl knew she was searching for the right words to express her thoughts. "Do not take this wrong, Cheryl Cooper, but the Englisch tend to be accusing when things do not always go their way. If the cows aren't giving milk, then it is Gott's will that they not give right now. We will sell them and buy a few more. We do what we have to do in the times that we have to do them. We do not look to others to place blame."

Cheryl nodded. She knew the Amish felt this way. "I understand," Cheryl said. "But I think you need to do something to help monitor the farm. It just seems that things are happening on your farm that aren't going on across the road. I'm worried about you."

Rebekah shot her another grateful smile. "Do not worry, Cheryl Cooper. Everything is going to be just fine. Instead of worrying about what is going on at the farm, let us worry about getting Albert home, ja?"

"Okay," Cheryl said. It wasn't the response she wanted to give, but when dealing with the Amish, it was the best she could do.

⁓⁂⁓

"Maam!"

Cheryl couldn't tell who yelled the greeting as six girls came rushing out of the house. Each one hugged their mom in turn, careful not to hurt her or pull her stitches. Then they gushed over Baby Yoder.

"He needs a name, ja?" Rebekah asked.

Abigail nodded. "I think we should name him Chris."

Girlie nudged her in the arm and shot her a bright smile. "That is because you are in love with Chris Borntrager."

Abigail gasped. "I am not!" Though the pink flush that rose into her cheeks belied her denial.

"Your daed always wanted to name a boy Paul, after his father."

Bethany muttered the name out loud and then gave a sage nod. "Paul," she said again. "I like it."

"What about Christopher Paul?" Cheryl said.

Abigail gave a small laugh. "The Amish do not always give middle names. Only sometimes."

Cheryl looked down at the baby boy, sleeping so contently in his secondhand car seat. She couldn't stop her smile. And thoughts about whether or not she would ever have a child rose to the surface. When she was dating Lance, it had never come up.

Well, that wasn't exactly true. She brought it up from time to time, but he seemed to never want to talk about it. Then when he decided that they needed to break up, she saw her chance of being a mother slip away. Despite Lance's efforts to reconcile with her at Christmastime, Cheryl decided that they should remain friends and only friends.

Of course, her attraction to Levi Miller wasn't helping one bit. It seemed to make her biological clock tick even louder than normal. Talk about an inconvenient romance. If she were to get involved with Levi—not that she was, because it would be so complicated—it would be years before they would think about having children.

She shook her head at her fanciful thoughts. "What I think is this little guy is so special he deserves two names."

Rebekah smiled. "Christopher Paul," she murmured as if testing the sound of the name on her lips. Then her smile deepened. She grabbed Cheryl's hand. "I like that. I like it very much. Thank you, Cheryl."

Cheryl could only hope that when Albert Yoder got out of jail he thanked her just as much for naming their child.

⁂

As the younger girls helped their mother and new baby brother into the house, Abigail pulled Cheryl to one side.

"Did you tell Maam about the missing milk?"

"No. But I don't know about Naomi." Then again, Rebekah hadn't mentioned it either way. That could mean either she didn't know, or it was such a common occurrence these days she hadn't given it a second thought.

"Is anything else weird going on?"

Abigail shook her head. "No. But you believe me, right?"

"Of course I do." The young girl was so sincere and earnest, how could she not?

"It's just—it's just that our family needs this right now. We have not been slacking in our chores. We've worked hard. Especially since Daed has been gone. We would not do anything to jeopardize our family. Especially with our new baby brother. But when you look at the missing milk and..." She trailed off.

Cheryl took the young girl's hands into her own and squeezed her fingers reassuringly. "I know that, Abigail. You and your sisters are good girls. And we're doing everything we can to figure out what's going on. But more than anything, we just have to pray that the benefit auction will raise enough money to get your father back home. Maybe then all these shenanigans will stop."

She could only hope.

"Abigail," Cheryl began. "You're not missing a buggy, are you?"

It seemed highly unlikely and impossible. Especially with Albert now in jail. How often did they use their buggies? The girls went to school, and she was sure that Abigail had gone into town from time to time, but that didn't mean she used a buggy every time. She could've gotten a driver. So as odd as the question sounded to her ears, she knew that it wasn't so odd after all.

"No." Abigail frowned. "I mean I don't think so." She gave Cheryl a hard stare then spun on her bare heel and marched toward the carriage house. For all intents and purposes, it was an Amish garage—a separate building from the house with two doors that pulled up on rollers. Much like a rolltop desk.

Abigail went around the side of the building and returned a moment later with the key. She used it to unlock one side of the garage then pushed the door up.

Immediately Cheryl could see the buggy sitting on one side. The side that Abigail had opened. Abigail slipped into the other side and came back out a few seconds later. She shut the door, locked it, and returned the key to its hiding place somewhere on the side of the building.

She shook her head as she walked back to Cheryl. "No, they're all there. Maam's buggy, Daed's buggy, the spring wagon. It's all there."

Cheryl nodded. Just as she suspected. But she had to ask. "Do you have a regular wagon? You know, one for crops and that sort of thing."

Abigail shook her head. "Daed sold the wagon a long time ago. Right after he stopped taking produce to market."

"Do you know who he sold it to?"

"Ja," Abigail said. "Of course we do. He sold it to the Dave Weavers who live three houses down."

"Isn't he the one who farms watermelons?"

Abigail smiled. "The best."

But if the buggies were all accounted for and the wagon had gone to another Amish family, then where had Justin MacLean gotten those she and Naomi had found at the farm?

The sun was beginning to set below the horizon when she left the Yoders' house. She had to admit it. She had fallen in love with this wonderful family who was having such hardships. She found herself wanting to do anything and everything to help them get through this difficult time. And she came away more determined than ever to discover who was stealing Albert Yoder's milk.

She was so close to Naomi's house she decided to stop by before heading back to town.

She pulled into their drive just as Levi was putting the Closed sign on the petting zoo and starting toward the house. He turned and waved, and Cheryl felt that little zing of awareness once more. Just seeing him again brought back memories of their dinner at the Chicken Pluck restaurant. Their evening hadn't been particularly romantic, but it was special, and that was almost as dangerous.

"Hi, Cheryl. What brings you out tonight?"

She got out of the car and shut the door, palming her keys as she walked toward Levi. "I just came out to bring Rebekah Yoder home, and I thought I would stop by."

"Maam is in the house."

"Thanks," Cheryl said, but before she could head in that direction, Naomi came out on to the porch.

"No, I am not. I am right here. Everything okay at the Albert Yoders?"

Cheryl nodded.

Levi moved away to finish closing up shop for the evening, and Cheryl breathed a small sigh of relief. "Rebekah is at home, the baby's fine, and the milking is done, but missing."

Naomi tsked and shook her head. "That is just a shame."

"I don't understand," Cheryl said. "Where could all this milk be going?"

She knew that where there was a need, there was a market. But how big could the black market for raw milk really be? Was it so important to have raw milk that people would arrange a rendezvous in the middle of the night and buy it from some man they didn't know? Wouldn't it be a whole lot easier just to get a cow?

But Justin MacLean wanted raw milk so badly he was circulating a petition to legalize it. He had a farm, but he didn't have milk cows. He had three cows, but they weren't milk cows. Not even for his own private consumption. Was drinking raw milk from your own cow even legal? She had no idea.

"*Ach*, Cheryl, it looks like you have a lot on your mind tonight."

"I do, but I came in here just to see you and visit for a little bit. And to not talk about the Yoders' problems."

"It is hard to do that when our neighbors are having so many troubles, ja?"

"You got that right. Have you thought any more about how Justin MacLean got those buggies?"

Naomi shook her head. "It is not like he could not just go buy one, Cheryl. Anybody can buy one."

"I suppose," she said. "But why would he want one? Or two. He has two!"

"I think that is the question we need to be asking." Naomi folded her arms across her front, her expression morphing into what Cheryl liked to call her thoughtful face. "Maybe he is going to start one of those businesses that take tourists around in an Amish buggy."

Cheryl shook her head. "The ones who do that don't really use Amish buggies."

"You are right. Maybe he is just planning on making smaller trips."

Cheryl crossed her arms and thought about it a second. "It's possible, I guess, but I just don't think that's it."

Naomi shook her head. "Me either."

"Do you think he stole the buggies?" She didn't know why, but the fact that Justin MacLean had those buggies and a wagon hidden in his barn bothered her. It made her feel like he was tricking them all somehow. Though she couldn't say how or why.

"You do not think he took them from the Yoders."

Cheryl shook her head. "I asked. Their buggies are all there. If he took them, it was from someone else."

"Do you think that is why they are hidden away? To keep people from knowing that they are there?"

"Obviously," Cheryl said. "But why does he need them?" She shook her head again. "I can't help thinking that if he wanted to sneak around in the middle of the night, what better way to do it than with the horse and buggy?"

Naomi scoffed. "Have you heard a horse and buggy come down the road? It is anything but quiet."

"I know, but in Amish country who would suspect? Then he takes the buggy around, steals Albert Yoder's milk, puts it in the back, and trots away."

"It is possible, I suppose."

"But not probable?" Cheryl asked.

"Why would he not just use a car?"

"That's just the thing," Cheryl said. "You heard Marvin. Sometimes it's a car, and sometimes it's a buggy."

"And sometimes it is a wagon," Naomi added. "I am just saying that a car would be much more efficient. And quicker."

"You got that right. So why would they even come in a buggy at all?"

"Maybe it is more than one person."

Cheryl shook her head. "It's bizarre enough that one person is stealing their milk. To think that two separate thieves would target the same family...?"

"Ja."

Cheryl twirled her keys on one finger and pressed her lips together. "Well, I guess it's just another dead end."

"Maybe not." Naomi thoughtfully tapped her chin with her forefinger.

"What do you mean?"

"I just thought of something. Did you see the back of the buggy in Justin MacLean's barn?" Naomi asked. "Right in the center of the caution triangle, one of them had a cross. You know, one of those raised sticker ones like Englisch put on the back of their cars."

"I didn't notice," Cheryl murmured. How could she have missed something like that? Maybe because it was bizarre enough to see the buggies there to begin with?

"And then the other has the sticker of a football team."

"A football team?"

Naomi nodded. "They probably belong to some teenager in rumspringa."

Now that was a possibility.

"So all we have to do is find those buggies in town and see who is driving them."

CHAPTER ELEVEN

Saturday turned out to be the prettiest day for a benefit auction that Cheryl could ask for. It was July but not too hot. A cool breeze blew from the north and seemed to stir things up just enough to keep them from getting stale. The sun shone, the birds chirped, and it seemed as if the day held more promise than any before it.

She had spent most of Friday collecting baskets and donations from the other vendors in Sugarcreek then making her own baskets to auction off. Now everything sat under the biggest tent that Cheryl had ever seen. In fact, there were three tents in all. All the food was served under one. There was anything that a person could want: hot dogs, hamburgers, chicken wings, and soft pretzels accompanied by more soft drinks than she could name. Under the next tent, long rows of tables and chairs stretched out, reminiscent of the high school cafeteria where she had eaten as a teen. Trash cans sat strategically by each opening flap, and once people finished their meal they could wander into the next tent where the auction was actually held.

Naomi had done an incredible job pulling the auction together under such pressure and short notice. Three auctioneers stood behind a podium, taking turns when they got a little tired from calling out bids. Rows of chairs sat in front of them, a variety of people milling around, English, Amish, and Mennonite alike. Everyone came to help Albert Yoder in his time of need. A large frame had been set up on one end of the stage, and a beautiful purple and white quilt was displayed there. It was one of the items up for bid on the silent auction located at the back of the tent. People came by and made their bid. Periodically the bids were posted to keep everyone up to date. Then a whole new crowd would swing through and bid on items as well.

But it was the verbal auction that held Cheryl's attention. She had seen auctioneers on television, but there was something about their constant banter, their trill and scatting that was so incredible to witness.

"I think we are doing well," Naomi said, nodding toward the table where the baskets were displayed. It seemed as if every vendor in Sugarcreek had turned out to donate something. It was a miracle and a blessing in one to see so many willing to help those around them.

"You think so?" Despite her optimism, Cheryl was nervous. They needed Albert Yoder home as soon as possible. Aside from spending the night in the Yoders' milk barn, which she was not about to do, she didn't know how else to investigate the strange happenings at the farm. Spending the night in the dairy barn was completely out of the question. It took only five or so minutes to become accustomed to the smells of cattle, barn, and manure, but she was certain that after a night in the barn, she might never smell the same again.

"I do appreciate you taking Rebekah home yesterday, Cheryl," Naomi said. "You have become a good friend to us all."

Cheryl squeezed Naomi's fingers. "I'm just glad I can help."

The next up on the auction was one of the Swiss Miss baskets. It was full of Naomi's jelly, honey from a local farmer, and a gift card with reservations for two to the Chicken Pluck.

As much as Cheryl wanted Justin MacLean to somehow be involved with Albert Yoder's woes, he had been the first one to donate to the man's relief fund.

At first she had wondered if it was a guilty conscience trying to make amends, but she had a feeling that Justin MacLean was as straight shooting as they came. If he wanted the raw milk and had been stealing it, why would he be circulating the petition? He served milk at the restaurant that was in a carton, and no other evidence pointed in his direction. Though the discovered buggies in his barn still gave her pause. And how he seemed to be everywhere at once. However, owning a buggy and being efficient weren't crimes. That only left his intense attitude about the sale of raw milk. Just because he was a bit intense didn't mean he was a criminal.

And speaking of intense… It seemed that Kip Elliott had taken the day off from the Yoder barn to stay at the auction and talk to as many people as he could reach without a bullhorn. Cheryl wasn't sure where the megaphone had gone, or maybe the chief of police and taken it from him when Twitchell found out he was going to attend the auction. At least it cut down on his obnoxiousness.

Still he walked around the tent handing out flyers on all the reasons why cows should not be kept in captivity and the dangers of methane gas on the ozone layer. Cheryl had to hand it to the man; he was persistent. If not a little bit wacky. The basket went for over one hundred dollars, and Cheryl tried to see who won it but was unable. The next item up was from the seed store—a new felt hat and a pair of insulated muck boots.

"That should bring quite a bit," Naomi said.

"Really?" She'd guess that most men in Sugarcreek would have hats and muck boots already and wouldn't need another set anytime soon.

But Naomi only nodded her head. "Hats get blown off into the mud, and boots get holes in them despite their durability. It is always good to have an extra pair around. And it is for a good cause."

The bidding began at forty dollars. Cheryl was shocked at the amount and even more so as the price climbed higher and higher until finally the bidding stalled. And the auctioneer handed down his gavel. "Sold! Number two-forty-seven." Down in front nearly fifty yards from where they stood, a blonde-haired woman rose from her chair and accepted the boots and hat.

Cheryl's tension immediately returned. That woman looked familiar. Really familiar. In fact she looked an awful lot like...

She shook her head and blinked a couple of times, trying to focus. Someone walked in front of her, blocking her view as the woman turned and sat down. So strange that she looked just like April Smith. But that couldn't be. What would she be doing here?

"Naomi," Cheryl started, "is that April Smith down here?"

Naomi's brow wrinkled and turned into an all-out frown. "I do not know April Smith."

"She's the sister of that young boy who was injured in that car accident with Albert Yoder. You remember the buggy, and he was in a wheelchair."

Naomi nodded. "Oh ja, he could not move at all after that, right?"

"That's right. He was a quadriplegic."

Naomi peered toward the front of the tent, turning her head this way and that as if to get a better look at the blonde. "I do not know. I cannot tell from here. Why?"

Cheryl shook her head. "I don't know. It looks a lot like her, but I was wondering what she would be doing here." It hadn't been that long since she had lost her brother. She could be just getting out to stretch her legs a bit. But at a benefit auction for the man who put him in a wheelchair? It just didn't seem feasible.

"She is a member of our community. Well, she lives close, but I know that she has been to town a couple of times before. And there is no law against her coming here."

"I know," Cheryl said. "But it just seems…" Strange? Weird? Suspect? She'd been watching too many old Agatha Christie movies. Not everything was tied up in a mystery. Maybe the girl just needed a pair of muck boots. Maybe the hat was for a friend. Who knew? But Naomi was right; there wasn't a law against attending an auction or buying the items she bought. Still, Cheryl wanted to talk to her.

"I'm going to go down there," Cheryl said. She started down the aisle, and Naomi grabbed her arm. "Why?"

"I don't know. I just have this feeling…"

"It is not our way, Cheryl. To bother a person in a time like this."

"I'm not going to bother her. I just want to see how she is."

"And you met her before when?" Naomi's blue eyes turned shrewd. The woman might only have an eighth-grade education, but she was as smart as a whip. "I think it is best to not stir up trouble today, Cheryl Cooper." The dancing sparkle in her eyes was enough to take the sting from her words.

"I just want to talk to her." Cheryl gently pulled her arm from Naomi's grasp and headed down the aisle toward the woman. Yet somehow in between making up her mind to go down the aisle and actually doing it, the woman had disappeared. She was nowhere to be seen. If Cheryl had even seen her at all.

"Do you know how bad cows are for the environment?"

Cheryl reached out and took the paper from Kip Elliott. His eyes registered shock behind his tortoise-frame glasses as he realized whom he had just handed his brochure to. He tried to take it back, but Cheryl was unrelenting. "Kip Elliott, happy to see you here today. I'm sure you came out in support of Albert Yoder."

The man sniffed. "I have not. I came out to warn these good people about the dangers of methane gas and cows in our society."

"And this work is for the EPA?" Cheryl asked. Beside her, Naomi gasped as if shocked by her forwardness toward the little man. But there was something about Kip Elliott that rubbed Cheryl wrong. She did her best to be a good Christian woman, but sometimes turning the other cheek was harder than people let on. Especially when it had to do with a sweet family who wanted nothing more than to live in harmony, raise their children and cows, and not bother a soul.

"So tell me, Mr. Elliott," Cheryl started, "why is it that you don't seem to be picketing Marvin Chupp's house?" She'd been dying to ask that question for a while now, and she seized the opportunity as soon as it presented itself.

Elliott sniffed again and pushed his glasses a little farther up on the bridge of his nose. Cheryl noticed that he had a Band-Aid on one finger and a piece of adhesive tape around the corner eyepiece of his glasses.

"I am not protesting anyone's farm, Ms. Cooper," he said with another sniff.

So he knows my name? Though Cheryl couldn't recall having had a conversation with him before. Who knew where he'd learned it?

"Oh? And what would you call it?"

"I am merely protesting the captivity of so many animals in one place. The methane gas produced by so many cows herded into one spot is unimaginable, and the danger it causes to the ozone layer is irreparable. We have to stop this nonsense now."

"There are fifty cows on the Yoder farm and probably not many more than that over at the Chupps'. So what makes Albert's cows worse than Marvin's?"

"Ms. Cooper, I didn't say anyone's cows were bad. I said they were bad for the environment."

Avoid the issue much? "Then why all the signs in Albert's yard but not in Marvin's?"

"I do not know what you're talking about."

"Yeah, you do."

"I think you need to give me my paper back now, Ms. Cooper."

Until that moment Cheryl hadn't realized they were still clutching opposite sides of the brochure, neither one willing to be the one who let go.

"I would think that you would want me to be knowledgeable on the reasons why we should not have cows in one place. Perhaps I'll find this to be informative reading for this evening."

Kip Elliott released the orange-colored paper with a wave of his hand. "Fine, I hope you find it enlightening." He turned his back to her, snapping his heels together as he did so.

"Mr. Elliott?"

He turned back around, the annoyance on his face painfully apparent. "Yes?"

"You wouldn't have anything to do with the missing milk, now would you?"

"Of course not. Sabotaging the Yoder farm will do me no good. I want the cows gone, not producing more milk. One thing does not have anything to do with the other. Good day, Ms. Cooper."

Cheryl watched him go, mulling over their strange conversation and wondering if she would ever get to the bottom of who took the milk from Albert Yoder's farm.

Yet Kip Elliott's answer nagged her all through the day. Just like the newspaper article about the Smiths from the day before, something in his answer didn't seem quite right. He said he wasn't trying to target Albert Yoder, but Cheryl didn't know what else to call it. He picketed his house, put up signs, used a bullhorn, had some sort of petition going around, and was now handing out pamphlets at a benefit auction designed to get Albert Yoder out of jail and back to his family where he belonged.

A new item went up for bid on the auction block. Naomi ran to get a number, and Cheryl let her gaze wander around the tent and to all present. It was remarkable how the whole community could turn out to help just one family. Honestly, if the English did more of this for each other, helping out and supporting each other, it would be a beautiful sight. There were Mennonites, some wearing conservative English clothes, and some who looked as if they were wearing dresses from *Little House on the Prairie*. Of course there were Amish and English. All sorts from all walks of life.

She let her gaze continue to wander around the tent. Remarkably enough, it settled on Marvin Chupp. He was standing near one of the flaps on the opposite side of the tent from where she was. He was standing tall, feet far apart and hands braced, as if prepared for a big storm to come blowing through at any minute.

But it was what happened next that shocked her. Kip Elliott eased through the flap, seemingly careful not to draw attention to himself as he sidled up to Marvin Chupp.

From where she stood, it appeared the two men were talking even though they were not looking at the other. *Hmm.* Very covert. Or maybe they were just talking to themselves. What were the odds the two men standing side by side at a benefit auction would talk to themselves? Or they could be talking to each other, and they didn't want anyone to know. She let her gaze drop for just a moment to keep them from being suspicious.

When she raised her gaze once more, Kip Elliott was putting away something white. Something wide and flat. Like an envelope. Like money in an envelope?

She really had been watching too many detective movies, but what else could it be? Was Marvin Chupp paying Kip Elliott to harass the Yoders? Did the man even work for the EPA? She needed to investigate that further. She had a feeling, as fanatical as he was, the young man did work for the EPA, though today's mission seemed to be in a class all its own. After all, why would the EPA want to harass one Amish dairy farmer?

No, this had more to do with Marvin Chupp than the EPA. But why? What did Elliott get out of harassing Marvin's neighbor? If not a little kickback from the longtime rival?

"You are getting that look on your face again," Naomi said from beside her.

Cheryl stirred then turned her attention to her friend. "I don't know what to talk about."

"Okay, then let us talk about you and Levi." Naomi gave her an innocent smile.

"There's nothing going on between me and Levi." Not without wanting on her part, but she knew how impossible a relationship would be and she wasn't about to rehash it with herself, or his stepmother. "And I don't know what look you're referring to."

"That look that says you are about to stir up some trouble."

"Me?" Cheryl batted her eyelashes innocently. "Why would I stir up trouble?"

Naomi laughed. "I do not know, Cheryl. It just seems to follow you around."

"Can I help that things just seem to get hairy around here sometimes?" And who would've thought that Amish country could grow so exciting in such a short period of time? She surely hadn't dreamed it would be that way.

When she accepted the proposal from Aunt Mitzi to take over the store, she imagined the tranquil community tucked back in the center of Amish country with a gift shop taking up her idyllic days and reconnecting herself with God filling up her evenings. So far it had been one mystery after another. But was she at fault for that? "Do you want me to help the Yoders or not?"

Naomi tsked. "You know I want to help Albert. Though I am not sure what that look on your face means."

"I just wanted a chance to talk to that girl. The blonde who bought the muck boots and the hat. What would she need with an Amish man's hat and boots?"

Naomi shrugged. "It is true that the Amish retain most of their followers. Most stay within the fold of the church, but we're not without those who have left and never returned. Perhaps her father was Amish, and she bought them for him."

"Perhaps," Cheryl muttered. It was as good of an excuse as any, but somehow Cheryl didn't believe it to be true. Why would an English woman need Amish clothing? It just didn't make sense. Coupled with the fact that she looked just a little too much like April Smith for Cheryl's comfort.

"So go talk to her," Naomi said.

"I can't," Cheryl replied. "She seems to have disappeared." She had been there one minute and gone the next. But if Cheryl saw her again... She was going to talk to her. If nothing else than to make sure that she was or wasn't April Smith.

"So how do you think we're doing?" Cheryl asked. She had heard about benefit auctions and how much money they brought in for all sorts of good causes, including relief in Haiti. Though she had no way to gauge if this auction was successful or not. They had thrown it together as quickly as possible, and though they didn't need an astronomical amount of money, ten thousand dollars was still a lot of money when baskets were selling for a hundred dollars and less. Every item was donated, and all the foodstuffs were donated as well. The day would be a sheer profit for the Albert Yoders. She just hoped it was going to be enough to get him out of jail.

"It's hard to say. I think we are close." Naomi frowned.

"Just close?"

"Ja," Naomi said. "I do not want to get my hopes up, you know?"

Cheryl nodded. "Just crossing my fingers and saying a prayer."

"What do we do if we do not get enough?" She voiced the words that Cheryl herself was afraid to say out loud.

"I don't know. I don't really want to think about it." With more and more people getting sick from what supposedly was Albert Yoder's milk, how could they convince anyone to lower Albert's bond? It would be next week before they could even talk to a judge concerning the matter. But if that was what they had to do, then that was what they had to do. "I guess we wait to see what happens. If we don't have enough money, then Albert can go before a judge next week and plead his case to have his bond lowered. It's possible that with proof of a hardship they might let him go home on his own accord, but it's hard to say. If people are sick and possibly dying from milk that they think he sold to them, then I doubt a judge would be willing to let him go anywhere, hardship or not."

"It is just not fair," Naomi said.

Cheryl drew back at the words. She'd never heard such sentiment come out of her friend before. The Amish didn't deal in fair and not fair, but perhaps it was different when talking about a friend. "I know," Cheryl said. "But we will do everything we can to get Albert back with his family. And as quickly as possible."

As she said the words, a movement snagged her attention out of the corner of one eye. With so many people milling around inside the tent, it was a miracle it snagged her gaze at all. But it did.

Cheryl turned to see the blonde-haired woman who won the muck boots standing in line near the ice-cream machine.

"There she is." She tugged on Naomi's arm and discretely pointed toward the blonde.

"That is her?"

"Yes. I think that's April Smith."

CHAPTER TWELVE

What are you going to do?"

Cheryl handed Naomi the rest of her hot dog and cola and started across the food tent toward the woman. All she had to do was keep her eyes on her. She would be there in just a second. Why would the woman run?

The blonde turned slightly to the left and caught sight of Cheryl. At least Cheryl thought she had. The woman took her change and was gone in a flash.

"Hey!" Cheryl called out to the woman, but she didn't even slow down. Cheryl picked up her pace, trying to catch up with this mysterious woman. All she wanted was a minute to talk to her. All she wanted was to find out if she was indeed April Smith, sister of the young man who recently died. Of course it wouldn't be bothersome to find out why the woman was here.

Of course *why* she wanted to know about the woman was still a matter of mystery. There was just something about her that struck a chord with Cheryl.

The blonde turned, and Cheryl could see that it had to be April Smith. But what was the woman doing here? At a benefit auction for the man who basically killed her brother? It was beyond strange.

April whirled back around and walked faster.

"Hey!" Cheryl said even louder this time.

The woman's footsteps quickened.

Cheryl just wanted a chance to talk to her. Just talk. So why was the woman running? Or maybe the question was why was Cheryl running after her?

She wove through the many people, some frowning as she pushed past. She could hear a few shouts of protest ahead of her and knew that April Smith was doing the same thing, pushing through the crowd, bulldozing her way around and through people to get away. What was the big rush?

She might never know. On the other side of the big tent, April Smith disappeared. Cheryl looked left, then right, then back again, but the blonde was nowhere to be seen.

"Sugar and grits." Another opportunity gone just like that.

"But why would she be there?" Cheryl asked that evening as she sat at the Millers' kitchen table drinking meadow tea and talking with Naomi.

"The question is why do you care?"

Cheryl shook her head. "I just don't understand."

"Maybe it is not for you to understand, Cheryl," Naomi said. "She is allowed to go places. Maybe since she had been taking care of her brother for so long, now she would do anything for a little bit of outside time."

Cheryl nodded. "I suppose you're right. But why wouldn't she stop and talk to me?"

"Why would she? She does not know you. You could be some crazed psychopath for all she knows."

Cheryl sat back in her seat. "Do I look like a crazed psychopath?"

Naomi opened her mouth to reply, but Cheryl shook her head.

"Don't answer that." She supposed she did look a little bit crazy, chasing after women she didn't know in front of an auction full of people. Something about the whole situation was more bothersome than she cared to admit.

"What difference does it make?" Naomi asked.

Cheryl shrugged. "I don't know. Maybe she paid someone to steal Yoder's milk."

Naomi shot her a look.

Cheryl sighed. "I know it sounds far-fetched, but I just want..."

"You want to help a family in need," Naomi said. "It is very noble indeed."

Cheryl shot her friend a thankful smile. "How long before we get the proceeds of the auction?"

Naomi looked at the kitchen clock. It was already after eight. "Probably not until Monday."

Cheryl tamped down her annoyance. They worked so hard. She would've loved to see Albert Yoder get out of jail before now. She had a fantasy image of her marching into the chief's office, handing him ten thousand dollars in cash, then marching out again with Albert Yoder at her side. Never mind that she never officially met the man and he probably wouldn't go with her. But she wanted to help the Yoders. And there was something wrong with the whole situation. "I guess Monday will have to do."

"They will not have counted it yet, and tomorrow is Sunday."

Cheryl nodded. The Amish didn't practice monetary transactions on Sunday. It was against everything they stood for to conduct business, even if that business meant getting a man home to his family. No, the best they could hope for was Monday. But the worst part of it all, she would have to wait till Monday to see if they could even get Albert Yoder out of jail at all.

Sunday turned out to be the perfect day to rest. After attending Silo Church, Cheryl came back to the cottage and slipped into some comfy clothes. But even as she tried to unwind, her body and her mind were going in circles.

Unable to sit still with her mind racing, Cheryl turned off the TV and grabbed a pair of shoes. Maybe if she just went for a walk she would feel better. Not much went on in Sugarcreek on Sunday. There were a lot of tourists milling around, but not a lot of shops were open. Most establishments closed on Sunday. Still, shopping wasn't what she had on her mind, just getting out of the house and getting rid of some of the excess energy that she seemed to have banked.

She let out a silent chuckle at herself and tossed back her head. If she remembered right, it wasn't a church Sunday for the Amish. She could drive out to visit with the Millers, but she figured that Naomi was still over with the Yoders helping take care of things.

Cheryl walked past the doors of the Swiss Miss, a sense of pride rising up in her at the sight of the beautiful little store. She may not have had a hand in designing it or opening it or even coming up with the theme, but she was more than proud to be a part of it now. She would miss it terribly when her aunt returned. She gazed around the street at Sugarcreek as a whole. She would miss all of it when she returned to Columbus.

If she returned to Columbus.

She wasn't sure what she would do.

She could stay in Sugarcreek. Maybe even continue to work at the Swiss Miss. Maybe she could talk her aunt into going on another mission trip to somewhere else. That wasn't fair of her, she knew, to send her aunt away just so she could keep living the life. But she so enjoyed the store and the cottage. This little town had come to be such an important part of her life. So important that the people in it meant more to her than any collective group of people ever had.

She walked past the pawnshop and waved to Wendy Hall and her son Drake. The pawnshop was one of the few stores that remained open on Sunday. Wendy herself had donated a beautiful basket for the auction and raised quite a bit of money. But even selling the baskets at a hundred dollars a pop, Cheryl was concerned that they only raised about half of the money they needed to get Albert out of jail. She turned around and started back toward the cottage again.

Unfortunately her short walk through the town hadn't rendered her any more peace of mind than she had before she left. So much so that she was starting to think she was seeing things again. Like April Smith across the street from her.

The woman turned down a side street, and Cheryl took off after her without a second thought. Maybe she could catch up this time. Maybe if she didn't holler out at her and alert April to her presence, she could catch up with the woman and find out why she was in Sugarcreek. Why she was at the auction. Why she seemed to be turning up more places than a bad penny.

Cheryl started across the road, waiting for a buggy to move past. Why she thought to check its caution triangle, she didn't know. Her gaze just went there as she crossed the street after the blonde. And there on the back of the buggy was the cross that Naomi had talked about.

Was that Justin MacLean driving? She had never looked. She turned back to where the blonde was quickly getting away. Then to gaze after the buggy that last week had been inside a barn at the Chicken Pluck Farm.

April Smith or Justin MacLean?

April was on foot and a much better target as far as she could tell. Silently hoping that she was making the right choice, she started after April Smith once again.

Fortunately for Cheryl, April didn't seem to realize she was being followed. Another half a block and Cheryl reached out and touched the back of her arm. "Excuse me."

The blonde whirled around. She had the same hair as April Smith and about the same build, but it wasn't April Smith.

Cheryl took a step backward, feeling chagrined. "I'm sorry. I thought you were someone else."

The woman gave a small nod. "That's okay." She turned around and headed back down the street once more.

Cheryl walked back toward the street where the Swiss Miss sat, wondering if perhaps all of this was getting to her. But she had gone after someone who was quickly becoming an obsession for her and let someone who was truly a suspect get away. Maybe she just needed a rest. But then she couldn't rest. Maybe she just needed a day of fun. But yesterday was fun. Maybe she needed something else. Maybe she just needed all of these mysteries to stop happening around her so she could enjoy herself a little more and not have to worry about her Amish friends getting caught up in one trouble or another. Or maybe she should just take a bubble bath.

She nodded as she drew nearer to the cottage. A bubble bath. Maybe pick up a book and read for a while. Get caught up in the problems of someone else. That sounded like a nice plan. Especially if she was chasing down strange women thinking they were the sisters of deceased boys. Yeah, that was what she would do. Go home, take a bath, and try to relax. Then tomorrow when they found out if they had enough money to get Albert out of jail or not... Well, she would cross that bridge when she got to it.

Monday came as a cloudy day. It looked like it might rain, though nothing managed to fall from the sky. As much as Cheryl knew they needed the rain, she would've much preferred a sunny day while waiting to find out about Albert Yoder's fate.

She was just about to break for lunch when Naomi came into the Swiss Miss. She took one look at Cheryl and shook her head sadly.

"Not enough money?"

Naomi continued to shake her head. "We only got about four thousand."

"Well, sugar and grits," Cheryl said. She had hoped for so much more than that.

"What do we do now?"

"I guess next week Albert can ask the judge to let him go home because of hardship reasons, and he might be granted that but..."

"He still has to stay in jail for another week," Naomi finished for her.

"Right."

"That will never do. They need him home now."

"I know." Cheryl sighed.

The two just stood there waiting on some beautiful, wonderful perfect idea to come down to either one of them, but it didn't happen. "You want to eat something? I was just about to have lunch," Cheryl said.

"That would be good, ja."

Cheryl let Lydia know where she was going, then she grabbed her purse and walked outside with Naomi. "Is the Honey Bee Café okay?"

Naomi nodded. "That would be fine, ja." Together they walked across to the Honey Bee, each one lost in her own thoughts.

Cheryl supposed they could try to raise a bit more before Albert got a chance to talk to the judge about coming home on his own accord. And what could they do but try and wait?

They walked into the café and over to the counter to order sandwiches and drinks. Then they took their food to a nearby table.

"Did you hear from Rebekah's family? Is anyone coming to help?"

Naomi took a big drink of her soda and sighed with contentment.

Cheryl knew that she didn't have soft drinks very often, preferring water and tea when at home. Today's drink was definitely a treat for her.

"Ja, one of Rebekah's cousins should be here this afternoon. They had church yesterday, and they have to wait to come until after they get their laundry done. Hopefully they can stay long enough to get the family through until Albert can come home." A stricken look crossed her face. "They will let him come home, ja?"

Cheryl shook her head. "I can't say for sure. I would hope so. It's not like he has a record or a bad standing in the community. But some of these judges can be a little harsh when it comes to certain crimes."

"But he did not do it," Naomi protested.

"You know that and I know that, but the judge won't have our knowledge of Albert on which to base his decision. He'll only know that according to witnesses, Albert committed a crime and because of this he has served time in jail."

"How do we find witnesses that say Albert did not do it?"

Cheryl almost chuckled. "We don't. What we have to do is prove that Albert wasn't the one."

"And witnesses would not help?" Naomi asked.

Cheryl took a bite of her sandwich then dabbed the corners of her mouth with a napkin and shook her head. "I wish I could say they would, but where are we going to find witnesses who will say that it wasn't Albert Yoder selling milk out of the back of his wagon in the middle of the night in the next county over?"

Naomi nodded. "I see. It is a difficult task for sure."

"Almost impossible."

"The things which are impossible with men are possible with Gott."

Cheryl stopped chewing. "You're right."

Naomi smiled. "Not me. Jesus."

This time Cheryl did chuckle. "So we need to turn to God." It wasn't a question.

"Always." Naomi smiled. "We will start a prayer chain. Maybe that will help."

"Prayer always does."

The ladies finished their lunch, discussing ways to keep the prayer chain going to make it stronger.

Despite the fact that they didn't have enough money to bail him out of jail and he would have to remain incarcerated for another week barring some miracle, Cheryl felt a little lighter in her step as she walked out of the Honey Bee Café. Faith was about believing, and Sugarcreek was a community full of believers. Now all they had to do was stand together and pray for help, and surely it would be received.

They started across the street when movement caught Cheryl's gaze. She turned as a blonde woman stumbled, met her gaze, then turned to the opposite direction.

"Was that...?" No. She was not running after April Smith again. Not after chasing her through the benefit auction and losing her then chasing her down the day before only to find out that it wasn't her at all. Cheryl was making a fool of herself over this curiosity, and she needed to quit. Immediately.

"What is it?" Naomi searched the milling shoppers who strolled down the streets of Sugarcreek. Overcast and sunny alike. Nothing kept the tourists away from the bright little town.

"Never mind." Cheryl sighed. She needed to let it go. Let it go and let God. Wasn't that what they said?

"Okay," Naomi said.

The girl who looked like April couldn't possibly be her. Yet she stopped at the corner then turned back. Her eyes met Cheryl's, and even at that distance Cheryl knew that it was April Smith. But Cheryl was not going to chase after her. She wasn't going to chase after her. She wasn't going to . . .

"That's the girl from the auction." She took off, trying not to run and somehow ending up at a full-out jog.

Smith saw her coming and whirled around to disappear between two buildings. Cheryl wasn't about to be put off. If she was going to embarrass herself, then she was there to do it wholeheartedly. She pushed down the alley between the two buildings only to find April Smith standing right there, not having moved an inch after ducking into the alleyway. "Why are you following me?"

Cheryl sucked in a deep breath. "Why are you running from me?"

"Because you are following me."

"Are you April Smith?"

April lifted her head. "Why do you want to know?"

This wasn't getting them anywhere. "Was your brother Greg Smith? The teen who was injured in a car wreck ten years ago?"

"Why do you want to know this?" But Cheryl could see the tears rising in her eyes.

"I'm sorry. It's just that I read about your brother in the newspaper, and it's very intriguing. I'm terribly sorry for your loss."

She felt like an idiot for following the woman. Why should she be doing it at all?

"I just wanted to be a part of the town. I've been trapped in my house for so long, not able to leave because of Greg..." She shook her head. "I'm just trying to get out a bit."

Just as she thought. "I understand."

April nodded. "I just need closure, you know?"

The light in her eyes seemed so sincere that Cheryl had no choice but to believe her. How would she feel if she were put in the same situation? She had no idea. How hard it would be to have to take care of her brother? Taking care of Matt would be heartbreaking if he had been in the same physical state as Greg Smith.

Cheryl nodded. "I'm very sorry for your loss," she repeated.

April Smith nodded. "Thank you." Then she walked back out of the alley, leaving Cheryl staring after her. She would like to say that the conversation was productive. But it wasn't. She had found out why April Smith was hanging out in all the places lately, but what exactly did she mean by *closure?*

CHAPTER THIRTEEN

With Tuesday's mail came the familiar yellow envelope. Cheryl was so happy seeing the pert and loopy handwriting that she almost cried. It seemed like forever since she had received a letter from her aunt, but it could only have been a couple of weeks.

She grabbed a letter opener and slid the blade under the flap, pulling out the letter, a huge smile on her face.

She was careful with the folded paper, only to have a picture fall out. She retrieved the snapshot and studied it. Her aunt was standing with two dark-skinned locals in front of a high water tank reminiscent of the Old West. Aunt Mitzi's hair was pulled back with a headband, and her eyes sparkled. Cheryl had never seen her aunt look happier than she did in that moment. And suddenly her decision to come to Sugarcreek and work at the Swiss Miss was the best decision she could've ever made. For all involved. Aunt Mitzi was happy. Cheryl herself was happy, and despite the recent disappointments of trying to get Albert Yoder out of jail, her time here had been fruitful. It had been productive, maybe even a little life-altering, but in a good way. She wouldn't change these experiences for anything in the world.

She picked up her aunt's letter and opened it.

My dearest Cheryl,

I hope this letter finds you well and everything is going smoothly at the Swiss Miss. I've missed Skyping and e-mailing with you, but our Internet connection has been very unreliable lately, so this letter will have to do for now. Every day I miss the store a little bit more, but then something happens that makes me realize what a wonderful decision I made. Coming to Papua New Guinea was the best thing I could've ever done. I've included a photograph of my friends and the new water tank that we just installed. It's such a blessing to see donations at work. And the good Lord has blessed us plenty.

It's hot here, if you can't tell, but in a good way. I hope the weather there is treating you well. It can be a little brutal this time of year.

Since the water supply has been established, we are working on ways to get it to the villagers. We also are working on repairing their huts so they can better accommodate this new luxury of water. Imagine that! Fresh water as a luxury!

Yet even as I write this, I feel a burden in my heart for you. I can't explain it and hope that by the time you get this letter that your trial is over. But whatever it may be, know that I am praying for you and that everyone here has added you to their list for their daily talks with God. I feel moved to tell you of Philippians 4:13. "I can do all things through Christ who strengthens me." I'm not sure exactly why I need to say this, but I do. If you're having trouble at the Swiss Miss, or trouble with your family, or just any trials in your life, remember that God is there for you. Jesus is there for you. And with them on your side, you can't be beaten.

Enough of the heavy stuff. Thank you for the last care package. You'll never know what such a simple thing as soap means to the people here. One cannot be blessed until they see the faces of those who truly deserve to be blessed.

Remember to remember us in your prayers.

Your loving Aunt Mitzi

Funny how God laid it on her aunt's heart to tell her that she could do all things through Christ. It was something that Cheryl knew always in her heart of hearts, but it never hurt to be reminded. Yes, they were going through a tough time, trying to help the Yoders keep the family running while working to get Albert out of jail.

But Cheryl needed reminding that God was in charge. And she just needed to trust in Him in order to have everything come out the way it should.

"That is a mighty big smile." Esther came up to the counter, a dust rag in one hand. "Is that a letter from your aunt?"

Everyone in the Swiss Miss knew that Aunt Mitzi sent her letters in bright yellow envelopes. She said it was the color of the sun and the most cheery color she could think of. These bright canary envelopes had become something of an icon when they arrived.

"Not necessarily good news," Cheryl said. "But news I needed to be reminded of."

"Ja?" Esther asked. "What is that?"

"That God is good," Cheryl said.

Esther's smile widened. "Ja. That He is."

"It's good to hear it again from time to time," Cheryl said.

"Speaking of reminding," Esther said, "Mom wants you to come to supper tonight. I almost forgot."

Cheryl smiled. She would love to spend the evening with her friends, but more than that, dinner with the Millers meant she didn't have to eat a TV dinner all alone. There were some things about being single that were always more fun, but being single and not knowing how to cook was the pits.

"I would love that."

Esther popped out her dust rag and folded it back into a neat square. "How about six?"

Cheryl smiled. "Better make it six fifteen. That way I can take Beau home first."

Esther moved away, toward the shelf on the opposite side of the store from where she had originally been dusting. "Six fifteen it is."

It was 6:21 when Cheryl drove her car over the charming old wooden bridge that led to the Miller farm. The Miller men were always trying to improve the bridge, and Cheryl was constantly trying to help them realize how perfect it was just as it was right then. So it creaked a little when she went over. She never felt unsafe on the bridge. And there was something about that bridge that seemed to mark a time and place of a long-ago world that needed to never be forgotten.

"Cheryl!" Esther and Elizabeth rushed from the house, both running down the porch steps before Cheryl even got the car turned off. She got out and shut the door, hugging each girl in turn.

"That was a mighty fine welcome."

Elizabeth smiled at her. "You do not come around often enough these days."

She supposed that was true. Here lately it seemed that she and Naomi were so busy trying to figure out how to help the Yoders, they hadn't spent much time enjoying each other's company and just being friends. It was a sad state of affairs when friends became too busy with other things to be friends. She made a vow right then and there to make sure that never happened again. "Well, I'm here now." She smiled at the girls and allowed them to lead her into the house.

Walking into the Miller home was like walking into her grandmother's house. There was a warm familiarity about the place that was welcoming like warm arms on a winter day. Maybe because things didn't change much on the Miller farm. The same blue couch, the same rocking chairs, the same grandfather clock, everything about the place held the comfort of sameness that she couldn't say existed many other places. She had once heard it described as "Amish time," and maybe it was. Things just seemed to move a little slower where the Amish were involved, and she wouldn't have it any other way.

"Something smells good."

The girls grinned.

"Maam made Levi's favorite tonight."

"Oh yeah? What's that?" There was a little part of her that almost wished that Levi would be gone tonight doing something or another. But then there was a greater part of her that was so glad he was there and that they were eating his favorite dinner.

Maybe she should go have her hormones checked. Maybe this unwanted attraction to Levi Miller was just a manifestation of "the change." Okay, so she was too young for that. But it sure beat accepting the blame for herself and knowing that perhaps she might be falling in love with the wrong man completely.

She pushed those thoughts aside and allowed the girls to lead her into the dining area.

"Do you need help?" she called toward the kitchen.

Naomi stuck her head out of the doorway, a dish towel slung over one shoulder and a pink flush on her cheeks from cooking over the stove. "Not at all, the girls can get it. Why don't you come in and visit?"

Cheryl looked back to Esther.

"Go on." Esther smiled, and Cheryl had the feeling she was being set up once again.

But when she ducked into the kitchen, only Naomi was in there. She couldn't help but breathe a small sigh of relief.

"The girls said you are making Levi's favorite."

See? No matter how hard she tried to push him from her thoughts, he just kept rising back to the surface.

"Oh, it is just oven-fried chicken."

"And that's his favorite?" Cheryl asked.

Naomi nodded. "Ja. But it is also Seth's favorite and Caleb's too." Naomi winked.

Cheryl laughed. "Then that's good enough for me."

"I went down to talk to Rebekah Yoder today." Naomi bent down to pull the pan of rolls from the oven. They smelled mouthwateringly yeasty. And until that moment Cheryl hadn't realized exactly how hungry she was.

"I thought we were going to relax and talk."

Naomi whirled around, pot holder still in her hand. "I am not sure how much I can relax knowing the trouble they have been having there on the farm. Did you know that their clothes are coming up missing again?"

"What?" Cheryl's eyes widened. "Again?" She had hoped that the first time had been a fluke. Now it seemed that was only wishful thinking.

Naomi pressed her lips together and shook her head. "I guess it has been happening for a while now, ever since you took those clothes back from Nellie Chupp, but it seems that every time Rebekah goes out to pick the laundry off the line, half of it is missing."

Cheryl shook her head. "That's bizarre."

"Ja. I know."

"Wait," Cheryl said. "Which clothing is missing? Is it Albert's?"

Naomi shook her head. "I do not know. But I would say no, seeing as how he is still in jail."

"Good point." Though she couldn't figure out what missing dresses had to do with the milk heist. If they had been missing clothing all along and some of Albert's clothes were missing too, it might stand to reason that whoever took them was also the person Cheryl believed was posing as Albert himself and selling the raw milk. But with Albert in jail, there weren't any of his clothes out on the line and milk theft had started long ago. "Is this the first time since we were there?"

Naomi shook her head. "It seems it has been happening a lot."

"Maybe we should go down to talk to them."

"Maybe," Naomi murmured. "Maybe."

As always, supper with the Miller family was a bright and joyous occasion.

After the first silent prayer, everyone lifted their heads and started passing bowls of food and platters of chicken around the table. Everything looked wonderful and very tasty.

"Have you given any more thought about a new buggy horse?" Eli asked.

Suddenly the clatter around the table stopped, and everyone turned to stare at him.

"What?" he asked, taking two more spoonfuls of mashed potatoes before passing the bowl to his sister.

"Nothing, nothing," Seth said. He took a roll from the basket and passed it across to Cheryl. "Biscuit?"

"Thank you," she said, not quite picking up on the meaning of the change in subject.

Seth handed her the peanut butter spread without even asking if she wanted any. Like she would refuse peanut butter spread.

"I mean, why should I not have a buggy horse? I have a buggy."

"You already have one buggy horse," Levi pointed out.

Eli made a face.

"Ja," Seth said. "And buggy horses cost a lot of money."

"Ja," Eli said. "But I have worked for it. I noticed that Marvin Chupp posted a horse for sale in the *Budget*."

Seth shook his head. "He has been trying to sell that old mare for two years now. I am not sure she would be fitting to pull a buggy at all with her age."

"But if I got that horse, maybe I could get another one to trade off," Eli said, his words trailing off as his father shook his head.

"That would be three buggy horses to your name then, Eli Miller. What would be the good in that?"

"I do not trust Rusty."

"You just expect too much from him too soon," Seth said.

"Then will you trade horses with me?" Eli asked. "You can have Rusty, and I will take your mare."

"I do not think that is a very good idea," Seth said.

Cheryl watched the conversation going around her, switching her attention from one Miller to another. Something was going on, and she had a feeling it had a lot to do with Eli's upcoming birthday.

"Give him a couple more months, Eli," Levi said.

Eli turned to his older brother, and for a moment Cheryl thought he might protest. Then he gave a quick nod. "Ja, okay then. I will give it a couple more months. But I am not going to change my mind. I want to start taking a girl home from singings," he finally said.

A round of laughter went up around the table.

"Oh, now I see," Seth said with a chuckle. "You want to take a girl home and do not trust Rusty to get you there without incident."

"You have to admit that it would be a bad thing if he were to run us off the road and I could not get my girl back home in time, now would it not?"

"Ja," Levi said.

Cheryl looked up just in time to catch his gaze over the bowl of green beans he handed her way. Suddenly the moment felt more intimate than just a side dish.

"Thank you," she murmured, accepting the green beans and dishing a helping onto her plate. Why did it seem that every time the two of them were together, something was brought up about dating, courting, being alone, or love? If it wasn't that, it was family and babies. It just seemed to keep coming from all directions.

The worst part of it all was that she knew it wasn't any kind of sign from God. It was just simply a cruel coincidence. And the quicker she forgot about her unauthorized feelings for Levi Miller, the sooner she could get on with... Well with whatever it was she was doing with her life these days. She wasn't going to be remorseful that she didn't have a special someone in her life. She had good friends, good company, people who loved her, and a wonderful family. That was all a person needed. Wasn't it?

After their meal, everyone bowed their head for another silent prayer, then the girls got up and made short work of the dishes while the men walked down to the pasture to check on Rusty.

"If he keeps asking about a horse, he is going to ruin his birthday surprise completely," Esther said, lifting the stack of plates into the cabinet.

"Ja, but that is between him and your father," Naomi said. "You just let him handle it."

"I suppose." Esther frowned. "Eli doesn't have any patience."

"What man does?" Cheryl asked.

The Miller women laughed.

"I suppose you're right," Naomi said. They wiped down the table and the counters and swept the floor then headed out to the front porch.

"Want to run down to the Yoders' and check on them?" Naomi asked.

Cheryl nodded. They still had another good hour or two of daylight. She hadn't been to the farm in a couple of days. It might be nice to see any changes that they may have made since the last time she was there.

"Do you mind driving?" Naomi asked.

"Of course not."

Cheryl fished her keys out of her pocket and got her purse from the house. She returned to the front porch just as Naomi turned to Esther.

"Go get your brother and tell him it is time to go."

CHAPTER FOURTEEN

L evi's going with us?" Cheryl tried to keep her voice level. Why was it that when she did everything in her power to stay away from Levi Miller, it seemed like he was constantly underfoot? Not that she minded. But she did. And yet she didn't. She definitely needed to get a checkup.

"Ja, I thought it might be good for him to check on the construction workers. We have been trying to go down at least once a day and monitor things."

Cheryl nodded, and they all piled into her little blue Ford. Thankfully, Levi sat in the back, leaving Naomi riding shotgun next to Cheryl. Still, the trip was a little bit too reminiscent of their evening out at the Chicken Pluck.

Lack of romance. That was what it was. That was why she was having such a terrible time remembering how incredibly wrong Levi Miller was for her. She just needed a little more romance in her life. Not that she was desperate enough to go sign up for one of the online dating services or anything. Anyone that she started to date in Sugarcreek she would end up leaving behind if she moved back to Columbus.

And there were those thoughts about moving again. They filled her with worry and dread. She would like to say that she would be excited to go back to her former life, but she had come to love life in Sugarcreek—its slower pace, its proximity to the Amish, the tourists... She loved it all.

In no time at all she swung her car into the Yoder driveway. Well, she eased it into the driveway between the herd of picketers who milled around in the street.

"I still think the chief should be able to do something about them." Naomi frowned at the sign-toting group dawdling in the right-of-way. She got out of the car and shut the door.

Cheryl did the same, and Levi followed suit.

"I was hoping that if we ignored them, they would go away," Naomi continued.

Cheryl shook her head. "People like that don't just go away. But I have an idea."

"Oh ja?" Naomi asked.

Cheryl nodded. "I'll tell you about it in a bit."

She had to admit that the Yoder farm was beginning to retake the shape of, well... a farm. The barn had been framed out, and it looked as if the concrete had been poured inside. She wasn't sure if any of the cows could actually walk through the barn yet. But they were making progress. All it needed now were walls and such, but it sure looked a sight better than it had the few days she had seen it before.

"Cheryl!" Abigail, Girlie, and Bethany all came running down the steps toward her.

Naomi laughed. "I have been coming down here every day, sometimes twice. But you come down, and they all want to hug you." She shook her head.

Levi chuckled. "You are not a novelty."

"I'm a novelty?" Cheryl asked.

"I don't think the girls get out a whole lot. You're probably their only Englisch friend," Naomi said.

"That makes sense." Cheryl embraced all three girls at once. Whatever it was, she enjoyed the companionship of the young girls and their sweet dispositions.

Levi looked toward the barn and gave a quick nod. "It is looking better out here."

Abigail pulled away from Cheryl and turned her attention toward Levi. "They're just about done. At least now we can bring the cows through there." She pointed to the end of the barn.

It appeared that the pens had been set up before the walls had been placed. Now all they needed to do was connect the silo and the door then wait for the grass to grow back. Otherwise, come the next rain it was going to be a muddy mess all over again.

"And the cows?" Naomi asked.

Girlie shook her head. "The same four still aren't giving."

"Two more stopped giving yesterday," Abigail added.

Naomi pressed her lips together and shook her head. "There is something wrong about that."

"Cows quit giving milk all the time, ja?" Levi asked.

"Yeah, sure," Abigail said. "But usually not six of them at once."

At the rate they were going, half the herd would be dry by next week. Something had to stop.

"Come on inside." Abigail tugged at Cheryl's hand.

She went along willingly, the girls hovering around her like bees around honey. It was a sweet feeling to be a novelty. She stepped into the house. "Rebekah?"

"Upstairs."

Cheryl followed the sound of her voice, up the stairs and down a short hallway to the door at the end. It was a beautiful little nursery, with yellow-painted walls and elephant wall hangings. Not at all the nursery she would expect to find in an Amish home. But it just went to show how similar the Amish and the English were after all.

Rebekah had just finished changing the baby. She wrapped the soiled diaper in a plastic sack and tied it up. Then she scooped the baby into her arms.

He was just so amazing. Cheryl could barely take her eyes off him. "How are you feeling?"

Rebekah nodded and swept a gentle hand across her son's forehead. "Goot, goot. I never did get a chance to thank you for making me go to the hospital."

Cheryl laughed, meeting her eyes just briefly before dropping her gaze to the baby she held. "No problem. I knew something had to be wrong. Some type of womanly instinct, I guess."

She'd never had children of her own. She didn't know exactly how she knew that Rebekah needed help. She just knew. Maybe that was just God.

"Well, I do really appreciate it. I do not know what we would have done had we not been at the hospital."

Cheryl nodded, her gaze drifting once again to the baby Rebekah held in her arms.

"Would you like to hold him?"

Cheryl nodded. "Yes, please."

She could hear the girls and Naomi rattling around downstairs, but all she could focus on was the little bundle in Rebekah's arms. Babies really were miracles.

His eyes were closed, and he seemed to be almost asleep. Cheryl felt her heart melt at the sight of this little boy. He was tiny, so sweet, so entirely perfect. And she knew in that instant that if she ever had doubts about God and religion, all she had to do was hold a newborn in her arms and all of those doubts would disappear.

He smelled wonderful, a combination of baby powder, Dreft, and innocence. She hadn't known that innocence had a smell, but it did. It was fresh and clean and made her heart yearn for what she didn't have. Would she ever become a mother herself? She didn't know, and in that moment she wanted to be a mother more than she ever had in her entire life.

She pulled him a little closer to her in a semblance of a hug then handed him back to Rebekah. He was making her biological clock tick a little too fast and a little too loudly to hold him for too much longer.

"He's beautiful," Cheryl said.

Rebekah smiled, smoothing back his hair once more. "I can't wait for Albert to see him."

Cheryl's heart went out to the couple. After six girls, he finally had a boy and yet he couldn't be home to enjoy him. "We've got to do something to get him home."

Rebekah nodded.

"Maybe in the next day or two I can take you into town?" Cheryl asked. "You can visit with him, maybe let him see the baby."

Rebekah's eyes filled with tears. "That would be good. I have not been able to ride in the buggy very well since the surgery. It just jostles me a little too much. But I am hoping soon."

"I'm sorry I just now thought to offer," Cheryl said.

"You're a good friend, Cheryl Cooper."

Cheryl smiled, feeling more blessed than one person had the right to. "It's easy to be a good friend to the friends I have."

They all went back downstairs and sat around the table, talking about their work on the barn and house. Just a little while longer and everything would be back to rights as far as the farm went.

"What about the picketers?" Levi said. "That cannot be good for getting work done."

"I think the girls have gotten used to them now. They just rush past them and do their work. The biggest trouble we have is when we try to leave the farm and they are standing there in the road."

"What I want to know is why they are not bothering Marvin Chupp," Cheryl said. It'd been nagging at her for a long time now, especially since she had seen Marvin hand what looked to be an envelope full of money to Kip Elliott. Okay, so it didn't necessarily have money in it, but it was an envelope and what else could it contain? Recipes? Doubtful.

"I do not know," Rebekah said. "But I do know this trouble with the cows is only getting worse."

"Have you thought about having security cameras installed?" Levi asked. It was unorthodox but not unheard of. The Amish avoided technology when it might distract from their work and God, but a security camera to make sure that someone wasn't sabotaging the farm would most likely be accepted by any of the less conservative bishops around.

"I thought about it, but it is just so expensive. With all the work on the barn and the problems that we've encountered. Now some of the milk cows aren't producing. Then the surgery and Albert being in jail." She shook her head. "There just doesn't seem to be the money for that."

Cheryl sat up a little straighter in her seat. "If we don't have enough money to get Albert out of jail, why don't we use that money to help you survey the barn and find out who's doing this to your farm?"

Why hadn't she thought of that before?

Rebekah blinked a couple of times as if trying to bring all of the details into focus. "That just might work," she said.

"We will have to talk to the bishop," Levi said.

"Ja." Naomi nodded.

"I can go with you," Levi said.

Rebekah's face crumpled with relief. "That would be good, ja."

Levi turned to Cheryl. "Can you take us to the bishop's house?"

In the car with Levi once again. Not exactly the thing she wanted to do most, but how could she not help her friend? "Of course."

Naomi opted to stay with the girls and help with the baby while Cheryl took Levi and Rebekah over to the bishop's house.

She pulled up into the drive, surprised and yet not at how much alike the Amish houses seemed to be. Large barns, tall silos, and beautiful flowers planted around a two-story white house that oozed tranquility and peace and made Cheryl yearn to just go inside and sit for a spell.

"I'll just wait here," Cheryl said.

Levi got out of the back and shook his head.

"Why?" Rebekah eased from the car, standing with a little help from Levi.

"It's just that he's the bishop." Cheryl said the words as if that explained it.

"And he is a man, like all others." Levi chuckled. "Come. I'll introduce you."

Talking with Bishop Ebersol was like talking to Seth, much to Cheryl's surprise.

He was middle-aged with a long dark beard just starting to show the first signs of gray. Twin dimples slashed down each cheek, and his merry green eyes sparkled behind the lenses of his wire-rimmed glasses.

"So you see," Levi continued, "if we put up some security cameras, maybe we can figure out what is happening on Albert's farm."

"And perhaps get Albert out of jail. And back home where he belongs," Rebekah added.

Cheryl had considered herself an interested observer in this conversation but couldn't help a small nod of agreement. Albert Yoder needed to be back at home. Maybe then some of this would stop. They had had enough trouble before Albert had been put in jail. Now that he was incarcerated, it seemed it just didn't stop.

Bishop Ebersol stroked his beard and gave a small nod, his glasses glinting with the movement. "I see. And what becomes of these cameras once a determination is made?"

Levi looked to Rebekah then to Cheryl. He turned his attention back to the bishop. "Whatever you deem needs to be done," he said. "We can donate them to the church so that if anybody else has problems we'll have them ready, or we can donate them to an auction for someone else's benefit. We could sell them at the pawnshop in town or a resale shop. Then we would take the money and put it in Amish Aid. Whatever we need to do. The main thing is that whoever is vandalizing the Yoder farm be stopped."

The bishop stopped stroking his beard and crossed his arms, the motion more thoughtful than blocking. "I see."

Rebekah and Levi waited patiently as the bishop seemed to mull over the situation. Cheryl shifted from one foot to the other as Bishop Ebersol rocked back on his heels. Perhaps that made his thinking go quicker, for less than a minute later he nodded. "Ja. I think that will be fine."

"Do you want me to arrange to have someone come out about the cameras?" Cheryl asked as they drove back to the Yoder farm.

Rebekah shook her head. "No, I think I can handle it okay."

Her answer surprised Cheryl, and the shock must've shown on her face.

"I can let my fingers do the walking," Rebekah said with a chuckle. "Is that what you call it?"

Cheryl laughed. "Eons ago, yes, I suppose that's what you did. You let your fingers do the walking through the Yellow Pages."

"Then that is what I will do." Rebekah folded her hands neatly in her lap. "I will look through the Yellow Pages and find someone to come out and set up the cameras. Thank you, Cheryl, for taking us out to talk to the bishop. You have helped us out so much, and we are grateful."

They pulled back into the driveway, and thankfully some of the picketers had gone elsewhere. Or maybe they were just taking a break. Whatever it was, Cheryl was glad to see that the crowd had diminished by half. It was a much more manageable number. Six or eight picketers were plenty enough.

"You go on in," she told Levi and Rebekah. "I want to have a word with your neighbor." She nodded toward Marvin Chupp, who had once again taken up his place on the porch. It seemed sipping lemonade and watching the woes of his neighbors had become his favorite pastime.

Rebekah and Levi looked as if they were both about to protest, then they turned and went back into the house.

No matter to her. She had no qualms about talking with Chupp about his role in everything that was happening on the Yoder farm. Despite his claims of being woken up in the middle of the night by cars, wagons, and buggies alike, she couldn't shake the feeling that he had something to do with it all—the missing milk, the nonmilking cows, the troubles with the barn, the problems with the manure drainage, and maybe even the protesters.

"Hi there, Mr. Chupp."

Marvin gave her a quick nod, but this time didn't move his position on the porch as she drew near.

"I see you have some protesters today."

"Ja. It seems that way."

"You would think that, but it doesn't seem that they are really picketing your farm, now are they?" It wasn't really a question.

"What are you saying?"

"I saw you in town," Cheryl said. She pointed toward Kip Elliott who marched back and forth. As always, his sign was propped against his hip as he shouted about the evils of captive cows into a bullhorn. "With him. What would you like to tell me about that?" Again it wasn't really a question, but Marvin Chupp chose to treat it that way.

"I'm not sure what you mean. I don't know that man from Adam."

"That's strange because I was pretty sure it was you he was talking to."

Marvin gave her a smile that didn't quite reach his eyes. "Do you not know? All of us Amish men look alike to you Englisch. It is the beard, you know."

"Right," Cheryl said. "Still, it looked an awful lot like you. Even looked like maybe you gave Kip Elliott some money."

It was a huge accusation, yet one she was willing to make.

"Even if I was with anybody, you have no proof about what changed hands."

Cheryl nodded. "True. But I intend to find out what it was. And if I find out you've been hurting these people..." She let her sentence trail off. Let him figure out what she might do in the case of him paying off Kip Elliott to picket in front of the Yoder farm. Some things were better left unsaid.

CHAPTER FIFTEEN

Cheryl picked up the phone at the Swiss Miss on the third ring. "Thank you for calling. How may I help you?"

"Guess what."

"Hi, Naomi. It's good to hear from you too."

"I'm serious, Cheryl. Guess what is happening now."

After dealing with picketers, broken water lines, manure problems, and babies who needed to be born with medical assistance, Cheryl was afraid to even guess. "You won the lottery."

"Seriously?" Naomi's voice was thick with incredulity. "The chief called, and he is going to let Albert out of jail today. Is not that wonderful news!"

"The best news I've heard all day." And it was. "And who do we need to thank for this good fortune?"

"The chief said that the judge lowered his bail. We made enough at the benefit auction to pay his reduced bail."

"That's fantastic," Cheryl said. "But what about the cameras?"

It had been two days since Rebekah, Levi, and Cheryl had been over to the bishop's house to ask about setting up the video cameras on the Yoder farm. Cameras were scheduled for installation on the next day, and part of their argument in favor of the cameras was to help them get Albert out of jail. What would happen to them now?

"I do not know. But it seems to me that if we can get Albert out of jail and find out what is going on at their farm, that is really saying a lot."

"I agree." But Cheryl wasn't sure how the bishop would feel.

"Can you take him out to the farm?"

"I thought you were just calling me to tell me the good news," Cheryl joked.

"Do you mind?" Naomi asked.

Cheryl laughed. "No, not at all. I was just giving you a hard time. I know it would be hard for someone to come in and pick him up and take him home. And it would definitely be next to impossible for Rebekah."

"Ja, that is to be sure. The chief said you could pick him up at about three thirty."

Cheryl smiled. "Just in time to get home for the milking."

At three thirty on the dot, Cheryl let herself into the police station, more than a little unnerved at how comfortable she was coming here.

"Cheryl Cooper," Delores said, ceasing the smack of her gum, but only long enough to greet Cheryl as she came in the door. "How nice to see you."

Chery wondered if Delores really meant that since it seemed as if every time Cheryl was in the police station there was more trouble than any one of them wanted to handle at the time. At least today she was only picking up Albert Yoder and taking him back to his farm.

"I've just come to pick up Albert Yoder."

Delores checked the clock and turned her attention back to Cheryl. "He should be ready to go any minute now."

As if on cue, Albert Yoder shuffled down the hallway with a thin young deputy at his side.

"It's good to see you again, Albert." Cheryl took a step toward him.

Albert gave a quick nod to Cheryl. "Are you my driver?"

Cheryl smiled. "Something like that. But really more of a friend. Are you ready to go?"

The officer handed Albert a bag containing a few things and his hat. Cheryl noticed the man wasn't wearing his suspenders. No doubt they had been shoved into the little bag of personal items. Albert also wore slip-on shoes, but he appeared to be in the same pants and shirt that he had worn into the jail nearly three weeks ago. Strange how time moved and how much had happened since then. It was just twenty days out of their lives, and yet it seemed that they had lived months.

"Come on," Cheryl said. "Let's get you into the car."

Albert Yoder turned out to be what most expected from the Amish. He was a little reserved around her, barely speaking as they passed things. At least that was what Cheryl figured his problem was. He didn't talk much, just looked at the outside as if he hadn't seen it in years. She supposed he felt that way. How did a man who made his living outside, who worked outside and played outside, survive in a small jail cell? She figured he was just glad to be out in the open once more.

As soon as she pulled up in front of the farm, the younger girls all rushed outside. They surrounded him, each one wanting a hug, jumping up for his attention, squeezing him tight and telling him how much they'd missed him.

Rebekah had come out on to the porch, baby Chris cradled to her chest. He looked to be snugly asleep, and once again Cheryl's heart melted.

Even with his girls surrounding him, he made his way over to his wife and son.

Cheryl felt almost guilty witnessing such an intimate moment as father met son for the first time.

Rebekah came down to the yard, meeting Albert and the girls halfway. "We named him Christopher Paul," Rebekah said. "I was not sure when you would make it home, and we needed to call him something."

"After my father."

Cheryl couldn't see his face, but his voice sounded thick with tears. He reached out one calloused hand and brushed it across his son's face. The baby stretched his arm out and beyond, even as his mother handed him to his father.

Cheryl was stunned by the gentle way Albert accepted his son. The big competent man seemed a little lost as he cradled the child to him, even though he'd surely held his daughters as babies.

"He's a good baby," Abigail said.

"It was Abigail's idea to call him Christopher," Girlie chimed in.

Albert lifted his head to look at his wife. "Is that what you are calling him? Christopher?"

"Chrissy P. seems to be what the girls prefer."

Albert chuckled and bent down to press a quick kiss on his baby's forehead. "Of course it is. Chrissy P." Albert laughed again, and Cheryl knew he was happy to be home.

He handed the baby back to his wife and looked to his girls. "It is time for milking, ja?"

Abigail smiled, her thankfulness that her dad was home evident in her sweet features. "Ja. Oh! Cheryl, do you want to help?"

Albert whirled around as if surprised she was still there, or maybe the surprise was that she had been invited to help milk.

"You've been helping?"

Cheryl shrugged. "Only a little. And only a couple of times. Your girls have done a great job taking care of the farm while you were gone." She was reluctant to say "in jail." More than anything she knew that Albert Yoder didn't belong in jail. That was something she would just as soon forget had happened.

She saw respect light up in the man's blue eyes, and she involuntarily straightened her shoulders and stiffened her spine with pride.

"You can stay and help if you want," he said. "But what do I owe you for the ride?"

Cheryl shook her head. "I told you once before, I'm less of a driver and more of a friend."

"Then please stay for supper, Cheryl Cooper."

As he said the words, the girls jumped up and down all chanting "please, please, please."

What was Cheryl to say but yes?

Once the milking was underway, Albert motioned Cheryl to join him in the milk room. "I have heard how much you have done to help my family. There is no way for me to repay you."

Cheryl shook her head. "There's no repayment necessary." How could she say she had gained more from the lessons she'd learned from the Amish than any payment could compensate? They had been just as much a blessing to her as she had hoped to be to them. Friendship, life lessons, companions, and more. She was just thankful for this time she got to spend with these new friends. Once again she thought about returning to Columbus and how sad she would be when the time came. Maybe she should start thinking about where she would live if she decided to stay in Sugarcreek. She had a feeling if she mentioned it to Naomi, that her friend would immediately build a *dawdy haus* out back. How funny would that be? Maybe they would start calling them Cheryl houses. She smiled to herself.

"They also told me about the cameras. Do you really think someone is trying to jeopardize my business?"

Cheryl nodded. "I don't know what else it could be." She pointed to the milk vat. "Have you checked it?"

Albert shook his head. He was at the door of the milk room and hollered something in Dutch. The only word that Cheryl understood was Abigail's name. The girl called something back, and Albert gave a short nod. "Abigail said that the milk truck is due this evening. Our milk vat should be just about full."

Cheryl looked over to the valve. Her heart pounded a little heavier in her chest. How much milk was truly in there? Who had been stealing the milk and why?

She swallowed hard. "Did the girls tell you that a few of the cows stopped giving milk?"

Albert nodded. "Six was the last count I heard."

Six cows from a herd of fifty were a lot to stop giving.

"There still should be quite a bit of milk in here, ja?"

Cheryl could only nod. She watched, her heart tripping over itself as Albert Yoder lifted the lid. The look on his face said it all. Cheryl peered over his shoulder to the near empty container.

"I do not understand. The girls promised me they were milking."

"They have been," Cheryl said. "I know for a fact. I was here even. Someone is stealing the milk, Albert, and we need to find out who it is."

But by Friday afternoon, Cheryl wasn't any closer to solving the mystery.

"I just don't understand it," Naomi said. The two of them had decided to take a couple hours and run a few errands together. She couldn't say that going to the discount store could be considered quality friendship time, but it was better than nothing.

"I don't know that we will ever understand it," Cheryl said as she drove through town. "But I would like to know why someone has such a grudge against Albert."

"You think it is a grudge?" Naomi said.

Cheryl gave a quick shrug. "What else could it be? Why else would someone want to vandalize his property, take his things, and then frame him for selling raw milk? Or worse, tainting the milk in order to make people sick and thereby up the charges against him?"

"You do not think...?" Naomi frowned, her voice dropping to barely a whisper.

"Think what?"

"That Albert may be feeling some type of pressure. You know, with the new baby and everything. Another person in the house makes for a lot more to do. More money to keep the family going." She shook her head. "No. Forget I said that. I do not think Albert would do anything like that. But I cannot imagine anyone holding a grudge against him."

"Not all people are as nice as I am." Cheryl laughed.

The frowned disappeared from Naomi's forehead, and she smiled in return. "Nor is everyone as lucky to have you as a friend."

Cheryl was about to return the sentiment when they came upon a buggy in the road. He was driving at a goodly pace, but that wasn't what caught her attention. It was the orange-and-black football helmet in the center of the safety triangle.

"Is that the buggy from Justin MacLean's barn?"

Naomi leaned forward and peered at the caution triangle. "It is! What should we do?"

"I say we follow him until we get to the straightaway then we pull around to see who's driving."

Cheryl's mind started racing in a hundred different directions, trying to figure out who could be behind the reins. But they were surrounded by too many hills and dips. She had to be patient until the road flattened out of it. It seemed like an eternity, but finally they hit the straightaway. Cheryl pulled her car into the left-hand lane. Careful not to startle the horse, she pulled up alongside the buggy and glanced inside, but she was too nervous about driving on the wrong side of the road to give the driver too much attention. "Who is it?"

"It's Roy's Abner."

Cheryl shook her head. "Roy who?"

"Roy's son Abner."

"And you know him?"

Naomi nodded. "Roy and I went to school together."

"Can you get him to pull over?" Cheryl's palms were beginning to sweat as she continued to drive in the left lane. Lately nothing was coming out as it should, and that was really making her nervous.

Naomi rolled down the window and stuck her face into the wind. She had one hand keeping her prayer kapp firmly in place. "Abner," she called to the young driver.

Cheryl was too busy watching the road to see how he responded to a car coming up next to him and hollering out the window at him.

"Pull over," Naomi said.

He must've agreed, for a few minutes later his horse and buggy were parked on the side of the road just in front of Cheryl's car.

"Hi, Naomi. Is everything okay?"

Naomi gave a quick nod and looked at Cheryl and then back to Abner. "This is my friend Cheryl Cooper."

He gave a quick nod. "I have seen you in the Swiss Miss."

"It's nice to meet you," Cheryl said.

"Abner," Naomi started, "we saw your buggy at the Chicken Pluck Farm last week. What was it doing there?"

Abner dropped his gaze to his feet and shuffled around in the grass at the edge of the asphalt. He kicked a rock to cross the road and finally looked back at Naomi. "I was having my buggy repaired."

Naomi shook her head. "Why?"

He shifted uncomfortably from side to side. "I sort of had a wreck." He raised his hand and started backpedaling. "Well, not really a crash. But I scraped the side of it. Well, I knew my daed would be upset about it, so I had it repaired."

"Without telling your father?" Naomi said.

As Cheryl watched her friend, Naomi crossed her arms and went into full-blown mother mode. "Why did you take it to Justin MacLean's farm?"

Cheryl half expected the young man to self-combust from embarrassment. A dark red flush crept into his cheeks.

"It has kind of gotten around town that this Englisch man MacLean will fix your buggy and no one needs to know about it."

Naomi met Cheryl's gaze and turned back to Abner. "You know anyone else who took their buggy to Justin MacLean's to be repaired?"

Abner nodded. "Oh yeah, lots of guys. I mean, a few of us have, I suppose."

"You know I should tell your father about this."

"Ja."

"But I am not going to," Naomi said.

Abner almost wilted with relief. "Thank you."

Naomi shook her head. "Do not thank me yet. I think *you* should tell him."

That deep red flush started creeping back into Abner's cheeks once again. "Ja, okay." He kicked at the rocks a few more times. Then looked up to meet Naomi's gaze. "Can I go now?"

"Ja," Naomi said. "Keep what I said in mind."

He gave a quick nod and swung himself back up into his newly repaired buggy.

"What do you make of that?" Naomi asked as they watched Abner start his buggy into motion.

He gave them a small wave as he passed, and Cheryl wondered if he would actually tell his father about the incident. Somehow she knew that he would.

"Well, it explains why the buggies were in his barn."

"He cannot continue to do this. He is allowing our children to deceive their parents," Naomi protested.

"How many of them do you really think won't eventually come clean to their parents?"

Naomi nodded. "Ja, I suppose, but I still do not think it is a good idea."

"You want to talk to the bishop?" Cheryl asked.

Naomi whirled around to face her friend, her lips pressed together in a determined line. "No," she said. "I want to talk to Justin MacLean."

Cheryl still wasn't sure it was the best idea to confront Justin MacLean about his role in fixing these teenagers' buggies without their parents' knowledge, but Naomi's expression was so determined that she didn't dare try to dissuade her.

"I think he might be at the restaurant by now." She pointed to the dashboard clock. It was two thirty in the afternoon. She had no idea how long it took to do things like chop vegetables and make chicken stock or whatever it was that he needed for his meals, but since the restaurant was between Sugarcreek and the farm, she figured that was the best place to start.

"Good, ja."

"What are you going to say to him?"

Naomi shrugged. "If he is going to be a member of our community, then he needs to understand our ways."

Cheryl wasn't about to argue with that, but she wondered how much the hippie-fied Justin MacLean would understand about the straight and conservative culture of the Amish.

They pulled into the parking lot, and this time Cheryl was able to park right up front.

"Not quite the crowd that they had before." Maybe today she would have a little time to talk to the man. Besides the whole buggy-repair business, there was something going on with Justin MacLean, though she couldn't put her finger on it.

It was as if he had taken to the town with a vengeance. The man seemed to be everywhere at once. Out with the petition, cooking dinner in the restaurant, walking through the tables checking on his patrons. How did he get it all done?

His hyperactivity shouldn't bother her, but somehow it did. It was disconcerting to turn around and see Justin MacLean everywhere she went. Not to mention him completely forgetting her from time to time.

She chalked that up to bad business etiquette and got out of the car. Together she and Naomi made their way to the front door of the restaurant. The whole place was set up to look like someone's house. In fact, Cheryl figured that it had more than likely been somebody's house at one point.

It was a sprawling two-story white clapboard with a gray-painted porch, white-painted posts, and green shutters on the windows. Cheryl took to the steps and knocked on the door. Naomi reached in from behind her and pushed the doorbell.

Remarkably enough, it rang. But why would a restaurant have a doorbell? Just further evidence that this had once been a private residence.

"Oh, it's you." MacLean opened the front door, but only enough that they could see a small strip of his face.

"Can I have a word with you please, Justin MacLean?" Naomi made to grab the door handle, but he held fast.

"I'm sorry, I can't talk right now. I'm getting ready for tonight's service. You have to come back when I don't have quite so much to do."

"I need to talk to you about fixing the buggies for these young Amish boys."

Justin shook his head. "I don't know what you're talking about."

"I have people who say differently."

Justin's eyes turned as hard and cold as flint. "Then you were told wrong." He started to shut the door. Cheryl leaned against it but was no match for his strength. Not that she would have truly forced her way in. She just wanted to talk to the man. In no time at all they were locked out on this side of the porch while Justin MacLean was still inside.

"That was productive."

"It spites me that he thinks he can come here and help our children deceive their parents."

Cheryl took Naomi's arm and led her back down the porch steps. "I know that's how it looks to you, but I don't think he sees it that way at all. Maybe we can come back next week and visit with him when he isn't as busy. And maybe we can head out to the farm this weekend to talk with him."

"Maybe," Naomi said.

They got back in the car, and Cheryl backed out of the parking lot that she now realized had once been a beautiful front yard of the sprawling house.

"Do you see that?" Naomi pointed to the side of the building.

"It's a side door," Cheryl explained.

"I know *what* it is," Naomi said. "Do you see that it is open?"

"Oh no," Cheryl said. She had been in enough trouble with Chief Twitchell. "I can't add breaking and entering to my profile right now."

Naomi waved a hand as if to dispel her protests. "I think that would fall more into the category of trespassing, don't you?"

"Do not split hairs with me, Naomi Miller." Cheryl said the words even as she started to turn the car around. Once again they were headed back in the direction of the Chicken Pluck restaurant.

Naomi smiled. "So you will help me?"

Cheryl shook her head. "I don't know what's gotten into me."

Naomi shrugged. "Just think of it as helping a friend."

They parked the car on the edge of the road just out of view from the Chicken Pluck. They needed to catch MacLean off guard. And that would never work if he could see the car sitting up front while they were peeking in the back door.

"I'm still not sure this is a good idea," Cheryl said.

"This is a terrible idea," Naomi returned.

"Then why are we doing it?"

"Because it is the only way to get the information we need."

Maybe she would like to have denied her friend's statement, but Cheryl knew that Naomi was correct. So far she had visited a restaurant, taken one of their menus, ate at the restaurant, visited their farm, snooped around, and now this. She supposed that was part of the natural progression of things. But she was still a little surprised with herself for her part in this.

They whispered as they walked toward the side door of the house. It was open with no screen door. For a moment Cheryl wondered about flies getting into the restaurant and figured that Justin MacLean was unaware that it was open. They naturally slowed their steps as they neared the door. Sounds came from within, the clank of pans, running water, and the *dunk, dunk, dunk* of someone chopping on a wooden block.

Cheryl eased closer to the door, somehow managing to peek inside without actually entering the building.

It appeared to be the typical restaurant kitchen with big stainless-steel tables, chopping blocks, a huge oven, and a large grill. For the most part, it didn't look like anything was actually cooking yet. Justin MacLean stood at one of the large tables, his back to them as he methodically chopped vegetables. His precision with a knife was miraculous, speedy, and efficient, and Cheryl was in awe of his kitchen skills.

From across the room, the door opened and Justin MacLean entered the room, his tie-dyed T-shirt stretched out at the neck and his petition tucked under one arm. "Jason, do you have tonight's menu ready yet?"

Wait. Justin MacLean was chopping vegetables. Cheryl swung her gaze back to the man standing at the counter. He stopped chopping, laid down his knife, and wiped his hands on a nearby towel. "Just give me a few more minutes. I'm thinking."

"Think fast. I won't have time to get the menus to the printer if you don't hurry."

Was she seeing double?

She wasn't the only one shocked. From beside her Naomi gasped. The sound was just enough that without the chopping noise for cover, it drew the attention of both men.

Yeah. She was seeing double.

One of the Justin MacLeans marched toward the door. "What are you doing here?"

"Why are there two of you?" Cheryl asked.

"I've seen you before," said the Justin in the chef's jacket. "You came out to the farm."

"You're not Justin MacLean," Cheryl said.

The man in the tie-dyed T-shirt took a step forward. "No, he's my brother, Jason."

Cheryl looked from one of them to the other. "I don't think I should embarrass myself by asking if you're twins."

Jason smiled, and Cheryl was glad they were dressed differently, for if it hadn't been for that, she would've never been able to tell the two of them apart.

"Completely identical, six minutes apart."

"But...?" Naomi started, however her friend couldn't manage to get whatever she wanted to say out of her mouth. She was just too stunned.

"Why are you telling everybody there's only one of you?"

Jason looked to Justin.

"Come on in," Justin said.

Cheryl looked to Naomi who looked at her. Together they stepped into the kitchen. This explained the mystery of how Justin MacLean seemed to be everywhere at once, but it still didn't explain why he was repairing buggies or what happened to Albert's milk.

"Justin, go get some tea. I think we owe an explanation to these ladies."

Justin did as his brother asked, and before long all four of them were seated around one of the tables in the empty restaurant.

"Does someone want to tell me what's going on?" Cheryl asked.

Jason took a drink of his tea and sat back in his chair. "We never told anybody there was just one of us. People just automatically assumed, and we thought we would take advantage of it."

"I get that," Cheryl said. "I mean I guess I do, but why?"

"It was for business purposes," Justin said. "How many times do you go to a restaurant and can't talk to the chef or the manager? It's frustrating if your meal isn't right or even if it's good. But Jason doesn't have time to come out all the time and talk to everybody about eating his food. He's got a lot of work to do."

"So you thought...," Cheryl started.

Justin and Jason exchanged one of those dual twin looks again. "We thought that one of us should be the front man and the other be the man behind the scenes. It's not like we're Super Chef."

Cheryl shook her head. "Did you really think this would work?"

Jason shrugged. "It worked for a while. As far as we know, it's been two months and no one discovered our secret. Until now."

"Promise you won't tell anyone," Justin said. "I mean, why would you want to tell stories on us like that?"

"I'm not about telling stories," Cheryl said. "But I don't think the people of Sugarcreek are going to like that you've deceived them."

"Nor are the parents of the Amish teens who have buggies you have repaired behind their backs."

Justin had the grace to blush. "That." He gave a sheepish grin. "That allowed us to get a little extra money and, man, did we need it."

Cheryl frowned. "Extra money? This place is packed night after night."

Justin nodded. "Yes, it is. But we're paying lobbyists to try to get raw milk pushed through the Senate, and that is a lot of money."

Jason sighed. "I told you to give that up. It's not that important. If we can't have raw milk in our recipes, then we can't have raw milk. It makes no sense running the risk of having someone sue because they got sick and think that it was because of the milk they were served here. It's too much of a liability, Justin." It seemed to be an old argument between the two. Justin pressed his lips together and managed not to answer. Cheryl had a feeling that once they left, his brother was going to get an earful.

"Tell me about these Amish buggies," Naomi said.

"It started off as just a fluke," Justin said. "One of the kids came to the farm. I think he might have had a couple of drinks. Anyway, he backed into the fence and then didn't want his father to know. I told him I would fix everything. He paid me some extra money, and I saw it as a good opportunity."

Naomi shook her head. "It is most certainly not a good opportunity. You need to have these kids tell their parents that they have been in an accident. Then let them decide who they want to fix the buggy."

"It's not my fault one happened there," Justin said.

Cheryl could tell that Naomi was not happy by this turn of events, but they couldn't very well make Justin come clean with his customers and their parents.

"So what about the milk?" she asked. "Did you have anything to do with Albert Yoder's milk disappearing?"

"What milk has been disappearing?" Jason said.

Cheryl had a feeling that the silent partner spent way too much time in the kitchen and not enough out in the community.

"There's a farmer whose milk was stolen and then sold to people as a raw product."

"You didn't take his milk, did you?" Jason asked.

"Of course not," Justin scoffed. "What do you think I am?"

Jason shook his head. "I think you're the kind of guy who is very passionate about raw milk and fresh food."

Cheryl stood. Justin MacLean might not be completely wiped off her suspect list, but she had a feeling he wasn't guilty at all. At least not over this.

"How about we make a deal," Justin said. "You don't tell anybody about this, and we won't tell anybody about your... excursions."

Cheryl shrugged. "Okay, fine." She didn't feel guilty about agreeing to his terms. The town of Sugarcreek would find out that there were two MacLeans soon enough.

Chapter Sixteen

Saturday morning came and with it the promise to catch whoever was stealing Yoder's milk. The problem lingered in the back of her mind, and Cheryl couldn't bring it to the front. It had more to do with just stolen milk and petitions and picketers. There was something big here she was missing.

She called out to the Millers' and left a message for Naomi to call as soon as she could. Maybe if they sat down and talked about it some more, whatever was bothering her would be brought into the light. It might not be anything. But what if it was? What if it was the one big clue that she needed to solve this mystery?

She went about her morning as usual, stocking shelves and selling goods to tourists and locals alike. That was one great thing about the Swiss Miss; it served both ends of the spectrum of the many people in Sugarcreek. Yes, she had great items for people who didn't live nearby and who needed to take a souvenir to friends or to display in their own houses, but she also had wonderful everyday goods that anyone could enjoy whether they lived in the area or not.

It was just after lunch when Naomi returned her call.

"I am sorry it took me so long to get back to you. It has been quite a busy day around here," Naomi said. Her voice sounded tired and a bit strained.

"Everything okay?"

"Yes, it is just really busy when the weather is this nice." After a couple of days of clouds and rain, the sun was shining once again. It might even be considered a little hot for July, but people were out in droves, shopping and the like.

"Did the Yoders get the cameras installed okay?"

"Ja, as far as I know. I have not talked to Rebekah or any of the girls today. I was hoping to run down in a little bit to check on everything. It is so good to have Albert home, ja?"

"Yes," Cheryl agreed. "I'm sure it is. Say, why don't I come out this evening and we can drive over there together? Maybe they'll have something on the recording. Some kind of clue."

Maybe she could figure out what had been tickling the back of her mind for a couple of weeks now.

"That is a great idea. Except how are they going to watch a videotape?"

"I think it's more of a digital recording these days," Cheryl said. "I'm not sure what they set up for the playback, but I can bring my laptop."

"That would be good," Naomi said.

"I'll be there after I get off work."

"Five o'clock?" Naomi asked.

Cheryl looked at the milling customers inside the Swiss Miss. If this held up until closing time, it would be well after five before she would get to leave. "How about six? I'll bring something out for supper."

It was around three o'clock when Esther came in, and Cheryl decided to take a small break. Her intent had been to work on paperwork in the back room and allow the girls to run the sales floor for a while, but as she stared at the numbers in the ledger and the invoices that needed to be paid and the accounting sheets where they tracked inventory, all she could think about was what she was missing in the clues to completely clear Albert Yoder. He might be out of jail, but that didn't mean he didn't have to stand trial for the alleged crimes.

At least for now he was out of jail. That was the main thing. They still needed to figure out who was stealing his milk and why. And who was trying to frame him for selling raw milk.

The smug image of Marvin's face swam before her mind. Of all the people who had the most to gain, Marvin Chupp was at the top of the list. An age-old feud over who had the best milk in a competition that most people didn't realize existed among Amish. Marvin didn't like that he was second to Albert Yoder. Nor did he like everyone knowing it. But she still felt as if she was missing something. Maybe it was the fact that Marvin had succeeded in getting Albert's farm to be a mess. She was fairly certain that Marvin was the one who called the EPA about the manure and had paid Kip Elliott to picket Yoder's farm. Why would he stop there? Would he go ahead and frame Albert Yoder for selling raw milk? It was a win-win for Marvin. He could bring Albert down and cut into his business as well. Did the man have that much animosity in him? She just wasn't convinced. Even though all the clues pointed to him.

She could only hope that tonight's recording would offer some sort of concrete evidence that Marvin was the one behind it all. How long could a man spend in jail for stealing someone else's milk and illegally selling it? She had no idea. But still, she felt a stab of conscience at the thought of sending the old Amish man to jail. She wasn't responsible for the actions of others. If he had hurt Albert, then it was only right that he accept his punishment. No sense in going all soft now.

"Cheryl?" Lydia stood in the doorway of Cheryl's office.

"Yes?"

"There is a lady here that wants to show her dish towels to you. She said that she has been making them for a while and wanted to see if you would sell them in the shop."

Another vendor. Business just kept getting better.

Cheryl stood and pushed thoughts of Marvin and Albert and stolen milk from her mind. Despite the woes of the Yoders, life went on. "I'll be right there."

⁂

Just as she expected, Cheryl wasn't able to leave work early, but she did manage to get out with a few minutes to spare. She gathered her things and started out of the Swiss Miss.

Once again, Kip Elliott stood where the Gleasons' corn maze would be come this fall. He had his bullhorn in one hand, his clipboard in the other, while his cronies marched around him in a circle carrying signs with their usual messages: Down with Cows. Save Our Ozone.

Cheryl was all for saving the ozone, but were cows completely responsible for it? She had her doubts. Maybe they should picket aerosol companies and factories that made cars with poor emissions ratings.

It seemed other people had become a little disenchanted with Kip Elliott as well, for there was no crowd around him.

The second best thing was that if he was in the Gleasons' lot in front of the old fireworks stand, then he wasn't at the Yoders' causing trouble. Cheryl could only hope that the lack of audience he had didn't mean that the others were in the road in front of the Yoders'.

She marched across the street, fully intending to take advantage of his lack of audience. As she approached, her lips pressed together in a determined line. Today was the day she would get to the bottom of this.

"Kip Elliott!"

He stopped midsentence and looked down at her. "What do you want?"

She dropped her hands on to her hips and stared up at him. He was on a little bit of a platform, raised up like a stage, strutting around like a banty rooster with his bullhorn and petition.

Wait, why did he have a petition?

"What's that?" She pointed to the clipboard he held.

"This is a petition to ban cows in captivity in the state of Ohio."

Cheryl bit back a laugh. "Are you kidding?" Maybe she should get a petition together to keep unnecessary petitions from being circulated in Sugarcreek.

"Do I look like I'm kidding?" He shot her a stern look that somehow came across more comical than threatening. Only by the grace of God did Cheryl keep from laughing. She wouldn't want to offend the man any more than she had to. She needed information from him first.

"Interesting." She almost choked on the word.

"Are you going to sign it?"

"I'm not a registered voter." Still true. Dodged that bullet. "Can you come down here please? I need to talk to you."

For a moment she thought he was going to say no, then Kip Elliott gave a small nod and hopped down from the platform. He looked back to the two young girls who were marching next to him. "Take five," he said.

Take five? What was this, a movie? Was the man even serious?

He turned toward her and crossed his arms. He left his bullhorn and the clipboard on the platform when he jumped down. Funny, but Cheryl had never realized how small the man was. He was barely five-five. She realized that every time she had seen him he had been standing on something—a stage, a milk crate. He spent most of his time raised up above others. As if somehow that could make him more important. Or more intimidating.

"I want to know what Marvin Chupp gave you the other day."

Panic sliced through his gaze, then he cleared his throat. "I don't know what you're talking about."

"At the benefit auction I saw Marvin Chupp give you an envelope. I want to know what was in it."

"I don't know who Marvin Chupp is."

"Really? You should, seeing as how you've been picketing in front of his house for weeks now."

"I've been picketing at the Yoders'. All that manure." He made a face and shook his head. "I do not know this Chupp."

"I don't want to call you a liar," Cheryl said, "but you're lying." She had a feeling if she pressed, then Kip Elliott would cave. "And you know what they say about lying."

"Why should I lie about this?" Kip sniffed.

Cheryl shrugged. "I don't know. Why are you doing this at all?"

"Because someone's got to stop the cows from ruining our planet."

"Marvin Chupp has cows. In fact he has just as many as Albert Yoder. So why are you taking money from Marvin?"

"I told you. I don't know a Marvin Chupp." He turned as if to climb back on the podium but stopped as Cheryl spoke.

"I hope it was enough money for you to hire more picketers. The ones you have now aren't very talented." It was a stretch, but anything to keep him engaged could also trip him up and lead to him revealing all.

He turned, his eyes flashing with anger and resentment. "How much money he gave me is none of your concern..."

Cheryl raised her eyebrows. "So you did get money."

Elliott crumpled like a wet paper bag. "So he paid me. Why should I not take money that someone's willing to give me to do something I was there to do anyway?"

"Because it's the wrong thing to do."

"Don't get all high and mighty with me. Cows are going to be the downfall of our planet. And you meat eaters need to realize that."

Cheryl wasn't sure how to respond to that. So instead she countered with, "Are you really with the EPA?"

He studied his fingernails. "Maybe."

"Maybe not." Cheryl surveyed him once more. At one point he might've been with the EPA, but with views like his she was certain that he was a member of a more radical organization.

"Tell you what," she started, "you stop picketing at the Yoder farm, and I won't tell anybody that you're a fraud."

He seemed to mull over her proposition then finally nodded. What choice did he have in the matter? None. Not if he wanted people to listen to him. Not if he wanted them to think that he was legitimate. And as soon as the Yoder farm was up and running, she had a feeling that Kip Elliott would be on to the next project. Maybe he would start picketing chicken farms. She could only hope.

It was almost six thirty when Cheryl pulled up into the Millers' driveway. Her stomach growled. Her chat with Kip Elliott had put her behind schedule, but it was worth it.

She had been driving out here smelling the delicious pizzas that she had stashed in the backseat. There were four in all, enough to feed all of the Millers before they headed over to the Yoders' to view the recording.

Cheryl slung her laptop bag over one shoulder then scooped up the pizzas into her arms. No one must've heard her drive up, for none of the Millers ran out to greet her. Cheryl made her way up the stairs then used the toe of one shoe to knock on the door.

The door flung open, and Eli stood there. "Cheryl, you know to come on in."

Cheryl lifted the pizza boxes. "I kind of have my hands full."

Eli's eyes grew wide. "Pizza? For us? Yum!" He took the pizza from her and headed for the kitchen. "Maam, Cheryl is here, and she brought pizza."

Naomi appeared at the kitchen door. "You did not have to do that. I have plenty of soup. We could have eaten that tonight."

Cheryl shook her head. "I wanted to. You feed me all the time. This was the least I could do."

A scant ten minutes later, all of the Millers gathered around the table. Pizza boxes were opened, and slices were devoured.

In that instance Cheryl realized just how fortunate she was. Not only had she met some fabulous people, they were just different enough to lend a new perspective to everything she did. She silently thanked God for the opportunities that He had provided her. She chewed her pizza down to the crust, what her brother Matt jokingly called pizza bones, and surveyed the friends around the table. There was not one piece of crust on anyone's plate. It was an Amish thing that she had just about become accustomed to. They ate everything on their plates, always. They did not waste food. Except for Eli, who had managed to pick all the mushrooms off his slice of supreme pizza, with the promise that he would feed them to the chickens once he was finished.

In no time at all, the pizza was gone. They had eaten off paper plates, and cleanup was quick and easy.

"Are you ready to go down and look at the recording?" Naomi asked.

"Let's go."

Seth headed off to the barn, and once again Levi climbed into the backseat.

Cheryl really needed to get over this crush she had on him. Maybe she should start dating again. Not that she was really ready, but perhaps it would give her something else to think about besides Levi Miller. Handsome, strong, completely-wrong-for-her Levi Miller.

The Yoder farm was almost back to normal. At least there were no picketers, no signs in the front yard, and most of the construction work was done. In the days since Cheryl had been out there, the barn walls had been constructed and filled in and the concrete had been poured and allowed to dry. It shouldn't be much longer before everything returned to normal. Once the grass grew back and the fresh wood was painted, it wouldn't take but another month or two before everything looked just as it had before. And no one would know that during the month of July the Yoders had experienced such trials.

"It is good to see those people gone," Levi said as he got out.

"What's even better is he won't be back." Cheryl smiled.

Naomi's eyes widened. "What did you do?"

Cheryl shrugged. "Just had a little talk with Kip Elliott. I told him I knew about the payoffs from Marvin Chupp."

"Marvin paid Kip Elliott to come out here and protest?" Levi asked.

"Yep, and I'll bet my last dollar that Chupp is the one we'll find on the recording tonight."

Cheryl had no sooner finished that sentence than the front door opened and Abigail Yoder came flying across the porch. "Cheryl! It is so good to have you here."

Cheryl accepted Abigail's hug, catching Naomi's gaze over the girl's shoulder. Naomi laughed and shook her head. She might be a novelty at the Yoder farm, but it was good to be welcomed and appreciated.

"We came to see if we could watch the recording from the camera."

It's only been installed for one night.

Abigail shook her head. "Everything has been going okay. No milk is missing. Nothing else weird has happened. Daed thinks that maybe things will turn back to normal now."

"We can only hope," Cheryl said.

"Come." Abigail waved them toward the house. "Supper is over, but we still have dessert."

"Unfair," Levi said, and with a laugh the three of them entered the Yoders' house.

Strange, but the Yoder home was beginning to feel as comfortable to Cheryl as the Miller one. If anyone had asked her a few years back if she would be friends with the Amish, eating supper and dessert, watching to see who was stealing milk, and holding benefit auctions, she would've laughed. Who knew that her life would turn out this way? Only God.

"Cheryl!" Rebekah said, drying her hands on a dish towel before reaching out to hug Cheryl. "Naomi, Levi, it is so good to see you." She stepped back to allow them access to the table then called over one shoulder, "Girlie, get three more plates. We have company for dessert."

Once again, everyone sat around the table with dessert plates and coffee in front of them. The younger children went off to play, preferring a cookie from the cookie jar over the slices of shoofly pie that the adults were served.

"I just wanted to thank you again," Albert said. He cleared his throat as if uncomfortable with the situation.

Cheryl couldn't blame the man. Most Amish men didn't find themselves in a position that Albert Yoder had. Doing jail time was completely uncommon, and then aided by an English woman was definitely unusual as well.

"There's no need to thank me," Cheryl said. "I was close and glad to help. So Abigail tells me there weren't any problems the last few nights."

Albert shook his head as his wife came back into the room cradling baby Chris against her breast. Once again Cheryl's heart melted at the sight of mother and child. She had always thought she would have kids by now. Yet envy was destructive, and she pushed those thoughts away.

"Do you want to hold him?" Rebekah asked the question even as she held Chrissy toward Cheryl. What could she do but accept? Not that she would've turned down the opportunity for anything in the world.

She sat back in her chair and accepted the newborn baby into her arms. The innocence, his weakness, the miracle of new life almost brought tears to her eyes, but she managed to blink them back with a small sniff.

She looked up and caught Levi's blue gaze. Gone was the merriment usually present in his eyes, and he watched her carefully as if trying to determine every aspect of woman and child. But if he found the answer, she would never know. He glanced away, turning his attention back to Rebekah.

"It is the strangest thing," Albert was saying when Cheryl was able to turn her attention to the conversation happening around her. "As soon as we put the video cameras out, all the shenanigans stopped."

CHAPTER SEVENTEEN

By Thursday of the following week, Cheryl was convinced that all was right in Sugarcreek. There hadn't been any other incidences at the Yoder farm. Kip Elliott had stopped petitioning and picketing about the cows. Though Justin MacLean still circulated his petition for the sale of raw milk in Ohio, there'd been no more sightings of April Smith, no more missing milk, no more anything.

She had just finished her lunch when the phone rang.

"Cheryl!" Naomi's voice was urgent. "You have got to get out here. The Yoders' milk vat is empty."

"Empty? Like completely empty?"

"Ja. Someone stole the milk last night. The milk truck came this morning, and there was nothing left inside."

No milk meant no money for the Yoder family. Once again Cheryl's protective instincts went into overdrive. "I'll be right there."

She left Lydia in charge of the store and headed out to the Yoders'. Naomi said she would meet her out there. And it would sure save a lot of time if she didn't have to stop by and pick Naomi up. As it was, twenty minutes later she pulled into the Yoder farm to find nothing. No chaos, no craziness. The barn building was complete, and someone had even laid sod around the barn. All looked well.

She put her car in Park and hopped out, barely taking the time to cut the engine off before she did.

"What is going on?" Albert Yoder turned to her and shook his head. "Everything had been going great, but now the milk has disappeared again."

"But we milked, Daed. I promise," Abigail said.

Albert gave a quick nod and walked out to the pasture. He ducked in between the strands of barbed-wire fence and approached the nearest cow.

Cheryl watched, baffled, as he bent down and pushed his fist into the side of the cow's udders. The animal moved sideways a couple of steps but otherwise seemed to not care that he was anywhere around.

Then Albert straightened and headed back over to where they stood. "I believe you, Daughter." He gave a stern nod. "If you had not milked the cows, they would be sore and full, but they are not."

"But if they were milked this morning, then that milk is gone as well." Cheryl looked from one Yoder to the next.

"Ja." Albert nodded. "That means somebody is stealing our milk in the daytime as well."

"We've got to watch that recording."

Albert nodded. "Do you know how?"

Cheryl nodded. "I can figure it out. Do you have the instruction booklet that came with the cameras?"

"Ja," Albert said. "Let me get that."

"And I'll get my laptop." Cheryl fetched it from the car then met everyone at the Yoder dining room table. She flipped through the book that came with the cameras, making a few notes about how to play back recordings and watch what had transpired on the farm.

"It seems there's a digital recorder that saves to an SD card."

She was surrounded by confused-faced Amish people. She smiled with understanding. "It's okay. I know what to do." She walked back outside and located the source box for the video camera and removed the SD card. Surely it would be okay. After all, what was there to record now? The milk was all gone. The culprit had moved on and wouldn't be back until there was more milk to steal. She took the SD card into the house and plugged it into her laptop.

"We only need to go back a couple of days, right?" She looked from Albert to Abigail then back again. "The milk truck came a couple of days ago, and there was milk then, right?"

The two Yoders nodded.

"Okay then, let me see what I can do." She started the recording. Everyone gathered around behind her to watch.

Boring was not the word for it. One of the barn cats wandered in then wandered back out. From time to time one of the girls would walk into the milk room then walk back out. Milk was poured, utensils were cleaned, on and on for two days. Which meant that everything was stolen that very morning.

Suddenly a man entered the milk room. Cheryl checked the time. It was ten thirty that morning. She paused the recording. "What were you doing at ten this morning?"

Albert thought about it a minute. "We headed over to Barnett's to check on some new cows." Barnett's was a farm just to this side of Holmes County. Cheryl heard talk in town that if a person needed it, Barnett could get it for you. And she supposed that was the best place to get new Jerseys to milk. Well, at least that would be her starting place.

"Everybody went?"

Rebekah shook her head. "I stayed here with the baby. Me and Gracie." Gracie was the second youngest of the Yoder children. The young girl was about three years old and wouldn't have been able to prevent theft. Not that she had been in the barn itself when the culprit came in.

"And everyone else went?"

Albert nodded. "Ja."

Cheryl turned her full attention to Rebekah. "And where were you at this time?"

"Upstairs giving the baby a bath."

"And Gracie?" Cheryl asked.

"With me of course," Rebekah said.

"I like to help," Gracie said. Then she stuck one finger in her mouth as if she had said too much.

Cheryl chuckled. Despite all the hardship, smiles like Gracie's made it all worthwhile. "So no one was around?"

"That's right," Abigail said.

Cheryl hit the Play button to start the recording once again. As she watched, the thief crept into the milk room. It was impossible to see his face from the big black hat he wore. A hat like every other Amish man in the district wore. There was nothing distinctive about the person. No limp or funny walk. He wasn't really big nor was he really small. The shirt was light-colored, most probably blue or green, which was typical for Amish men. Black suspenders, black broadfall pants. The only thing that stuck out to Cheryl was that he seemed to have lost some weight. Or else had borrowed clothes from someone.

Then like an explosion inside her brain, that fact that had been niggling at Cheryl since this whole debacle started thrust forth into the light.

"You said you had clothes missing."

Albert nodded. "Ja. All kinds of clothes."

"Have any disappeared since you've been home?"

Albert nodded.

"Men's clothes?" Cheryl asked.

"Ja, and a few I had gotten for the baby and a couple of dresses."

"What about a hat?"

"I was missing one for a while."

"Did you find it?" Cheryl asked.

"Ja, I did," Abigail said. "A lot of things were missing then turned back up."

"A pair of boots?"

"Ja." Abigail frowned. "Does that have something to do with it?"

"I'm afraid it does." She'd been so blind. She had been so wrapped up in trying to prove that Marvin Chupp was guilty that she hadn't even considered anyone else for long.

"So you know who is stealing the milk?" Albert Yoder asked.

"Yes," Cheryl said. "I think I do."

As she said the words, a rumbling murmur went up around the table.

"Who? Who?" was spoken over and over.

Cheryl was just about to explain when Bethany ran back into the house. "Come! Come quick! The barn is on fire!"

CHAPTER EIGHTEEN

Hadn't she just felt that things had returned to normal at the Yoder farm?

They ran outside to see orange flames licking at the new roof.

Cheryl ran back into the house and grabbed her purse, snatching up her cell phone and dialing 911 with shaking fingers.

She explained as best she could that the barn was on fire at the Yoder farm, but knew that they had to do something there. She raced back outside just as Albert and Abigail were pulling the hoses around. Thankfully, all the cows were in the pasture and the heat from the blaze pushed them farther away. They stood in a semicircle watching as the humans ran around doing everything in their power to stop the blaze.

Through the smoke and panic, Cheryl turned just in time to see a buggy whiz past. It was going way too fast for a casual afternoon drive, and with the way the Amish love to help each other, why didn't it stop? Only one answer to that.

Cheryl tugged on Naomi's sleeve and pointed toward the departing buggy. "I think there goes our arsonist right there."

Naomi headed toward her buggy as if to chase after her, but Cheryl pointed toward her car. "Let's go."

They hopped into the Ford as the Yoders continued to battle the fire. Cheryl couldn't let the person responsible get away.

The cornstalks were just high enough that she couldn't see around any of the turns, which cost them time. Yet she was determined. Stealing milk and false accusations were one thing, but setting fire to the barn? This was no casual feud. This was serious.

She said a silent prayer that the Yoders were having great success putting out the fire and that fire trucks from town would be there soon. Such a shame the brand-new barn would burn just like that.

"There he is," Naomi pointed toward the left, down another road surrounded on either side by cornstalks. It was a little like heading through a tunnel, driving between all the green stalks of corn. Around the bend, the buggy picked up more speed.

I can't let that buggy get away. Cheryl pushed the accelerator harder, more concerned with darting animals and children scootering on the side of the road than she was about her own safety. They weren't going incredibly fast, but too fast to slow down should they encounter a pedestrian.

Thankfully they had a straightaway, and Cheryl felt a little more comfortable speeding up. She pressed the accelerator to the floorboard.

Beside her, in the passenger seat, Naomi held on for dear life. She had one hand braced against the dash and the fingers of the other curled around the door handle as if that would somehow keep her in place.

"Here we go!" Cheryl pulled around the buggy, taking quick note of the white lather already building up on the horse's flanks. She pulled ahead just a couple more yards... Just a little bit farther and...

"Brace yourself!"

Cheryl hit the brake, sending the car lurching sideways only to come to a stop sideways in the road.

The buggy driver pulled back hard on the reins. Cheryl didn't have much chance to note who was driving. Instinctively, she covered her head with her hands and braced herself for impact. She said a small prayer that she had left enough room between her and him before her daredevil tactic.

Lord, please let it be enough. Let the horse be okay. Don't let the buggy hit us. Please keep us safe.

There was a shuddering rattle, the whinny of the horse, then the dull thud of the locked wheels against the pavement. Then everything seemed to go silent. Cheryl lifted her hands from her head, taking quick note that they were all in one piece.

She got out of the car, staring across the hood toward the buggy driver.

"April Smith!"

The young woman was dressed in an Amish frock and apron with a prayer kapp completing the look. Cheryl had been around Naomi and her girls enough to realize that pieces of her outfit weren't quite right. Her kapp was pinned a little too far back on her head. The apron looked to be wrong side out and not one that was worn during the week. Still, it was a good enough disguise to fool the casual passerby. And went a long way in explaining how April had pulled off some of the feats she had.

"Oh no." April tossed the reins onto the horse's back and climbed down from the buggy as quickly as she could. Thankfully climbing in and out of an Amish buggy was not the most graceful endeavor. According to Naomi, even those who had a lifetime of practice sometimes struggled to get out without feeling as if they were going to tip the buggy completely over.

April stumbled, catching a foot in the buggy as the other one searched for solid ground. The horse danced from side to side as she worked to free herself.

Cheryl barreled around her car in an instant. April Smith couldn't get away.

April managed to clear her foot and take off running across the road and into a nearby cornfield.

She was just short enough that only the top of her white prayer kapp was visible as she raced through the stalks.

Without thinking twice Cheryl took off after her.

"Cheryl! Where are you going?"

She could hear the rustle of April in front of her and the steady footsteps of Naomi behind. Whatever the cost, she couldn't let April get away. She had done so much damage to everyone's lives. She had landed Albert in jail for nearly three weeks and sold tainted milk that made people deathly sick. No, she could not be allowed to escape.

But the cornstalks were playing tricks on Cheryl's ears. What sounded like it had come from in front of her now was coming from the side. She jumped a little higher, thankful to be tall enough to see over the cornstalks.

But maybe the corn wasn't playing tricks on her after all. April Smith had swung back around and had started back toward the road. Cheryl took off behind her, still intent on catching the girl.

"Naomi," she yelled.

"I'm here."

Cheryl had no idea where "here" was, but as long as Naomi was close that was all that mattered.

"Go back to my car and get my cell phone. We need to call the chief."

"Ja."

Now Cheryl had to deal with two sets of rustling sounds in the cornstalks. Naomi was on her left. Which meant the rustle on her right had to be April Smith.

She pushed her way through the cornstalks, the leaves sticky and cutting at her hands as she did so. April had to be close. *Lord, please let her be close.* She crashed through one side of the cornfield only to find herself back in the road.

Once again, April Smith was trying to get back into her buggy.

Naomi emerged next to her only seconds later.

Cheryl looked from April back to Naomi. "Get the phone!"

Naomi nodded and ran for the car while Cheryl went after April. Thankfully getting into a buggy was even harder than getting out of one. Cheryl snaked one arm around her waist. She wasn't sure exactly how she would subdue April until the chief got there, but surely she and Naomi could think of something.

But the girl fought with all her might, pummeling Cheryl's arm as she tried to hang on to her. "Let me go! Let me go!"

"Not on your life." But Cheryl's arms were getting tired, and in no time at all her grip slipped. April Smith hit the ground and started running down the road. This time, however, she didn't dash into the cornfield. She just ran straight down the line. Her steps were awkward and slow as if she were getting more tired by the second.

Still, Cheryl couldn't let her escape. She took off after April, running down the road just behind her. She stopped as around the bend Chief Twitchell pulled his patrol vehicle to a stop just ahead.

By the time they got back to the Yoders' place, there wasn't much left of the barn. This time though, instead of it being the back half where the holding pens were, it was the entire barn. All the concrete slabs and the metal dividers still remained. Along with the milk vat and the large stainless-steel sink. Both were covered in soot, and both would most likely have to be replaced. But thankfully no one was hurt. That was the biggest blessing of all.

"I still do not quite understand." Rebekah Yoder bounced baby Chris against her shoulder and gently rubbed his back. She looked from her husband to Cheryl then to the chief and back again.

April Smith had been taken away by one of the other uniformed officers and placed under arrest for the sale of raw milk, breaking and entering, grand larceny, and a host of other charges to encompass all of her crimes.

The chief looked to Cheryl. "You want to try to explain?"

Cheryl thought about it a moment then gave a quick nod. "Not everyone lives by the Golden Rule," she said, thinking that would be the best way to introduce the concept of revenge. Of course the Amish knew what revenge was, but it was a totally foreign concept to them. The Amish didn't live on revenge. They lived on forgiveness.

"As far as I can tell, April felt like her brother died twice. He died when he became a quadriplegic and was unable to move for ten years. Then he died again when his soul actually left the earth. April had spent so much time taking care of him that she grew bitter and lonely. She resented the fact that Albert didn't have to pay for what she considered to be his crime."

"I did nothing wrong," Albert said.

"We know that," Cheryl said. "But it's hard when you're hurt to see the truth as it really is."

Albert Yoder hadn't been doing anything wrong as he tried to get his rig to the side of the road that night. His lights were flashing, and he had his slow-moving vehicle sign. It wasn't his fault or responsibility that Greg Smith was driving way too fast and possibly drinking. It wasn't his fault that he came around the corner too quickly or that he wasn't wearing his seat belt and was thrown from the car. If any of those factors had been removed, the chances were that Greg would be alive and possibly even uninjured today. But those factors were in place. April resented it.

"What will happen to April now?" Naomi asked.

The chief shrugged. "That'll be up to the judge. But chances are she'll spend a long time in jail for her role in these crimes. It's one thing to commit a crime on your own, but quite another to commit a crime and frame someone innocent for it."

"Will we be able to visit with her?" Rebekah asked.

If the chief was completely taken aback, he didn't show it. Just a small light of surprise shone in his eyes as he gave a small nod. "If she's not opposed to it, then I don't see why not."

Rebekah smiled as she continued to pat baby Chris on the back. "I think it is important that she knows we forgive her."

"Ja," Albert said.

And once again the unbelievable charity of the Amish melted Cheryl's heart. Who else would forgive someone so easily? April Smith was responsible for Albert Yoder spending three weeks in jail and missing his son's birth. She stole milk from them, took their clothes, and vandalized their property, then she had burned down their barn. And they wanted her to know that they forgave her.

Suddenly Cheryl knew why she wanted to stay so close to her friends here in Sugarcreek. It wasn't everywhere that a person could learn such beautiful lessons in life as they could when they were next to the Amish.

And there were still so many lessons that she could learn.

An hour or so later the chief hopped into his patrol car and sped away. Naomi looked back to the smoldering remains of the barn and shook her head.

"I know," Albert said. "It is time to rebuild. Again."

Despite everything they had been through, Rebekah smiled. "It will be all right, Husband."

He gazed around the farm and looked up at the sky then gave a small nod. "Ja. It will."

"Come on. Let us have some tea," Abigail said.

Once again, Cheryl was brought into the bosom of the family that she never dreamed she would ever meet. They all gathered around the table with glasses of meadow tea and a large plate of sugar cookies that Abigail had made the day before.

"I am so glad you came to help us, Cheryl Cooper," Rebekah said. She reached a hand across the table and squeezed Cheryl's fingers lightly.

Cheryl's heart burst with joy. It was one thing to know that Aunt Mitzi was out living her dream of helping people in a faraway place while she was here. But to know that she had brought change and perhaps been a support to her new friends was an added bonus.

"I'm so very glad to be here." She smiled at Rebekah.

"I think we should have a cookout," Albert said.

"A cookout?" Cheryl asked.

"Ja," Albert said.

Naomi clapped her hands together.

"That is a wonderful idea," Rebekah said.

Abigail hopped up from the table and went over to the sideboard and pulled out some paper and a pen. "I will make a list of what we will need."

Cheryl smiled and promised to bring potato salad and a bag of chips. Then she said a small prayer for blessings and miracles and thanked God for them both.

Since the following Sunday was a nonchurch Sunday for the Amish community, everyone decided it was the perfect day to get together for their cookout. Cheryl promised to be there just as soon as the Silo Church let out. She went by her cottage to pick up the potato salad.

She unlocked the cottage and hurried inside, quickly changing clothes and grabbing the potato salad and the bags of chips before hustling back out the door. She stopped to give Beau a quick pat on the head then caught sight of the yellow envelope containing Aunt Mitzi's last letter lying on the coffee table.

"'I can do all things through Christ who strengthens me,'" she quoted. She never would've thought she would chase down a burglar or run through a cornfield after one, or even pull her car around to stop someone from fleeing. But God had been with her every step of the way.

"Thank You," she said and made a note that she should thank God more often for the strength He gave her, as well as the friends and the opportunities she had found here in Sugarcreek.

The cookout was in full swing by the time she got to the Yoders' house. Never ones to procrastinate or put off, the Yoders had already torn down the old barn and started framing a new one.

Cheryl had caught wind through the Amish grapevine that on Saturday they held a small barn raising to help Albert Yoder get himself back on his feet. The entire structure was framed, and it appeared that all they needed to do now was build the interior walls and paint. It seemed that things went much easier when the Amish were the only ones involved. Or maybe it was just because there was no concrete, no broken pipes, and no heavy earth-moving equipment involved this time.

She parked her car and got out, waiting as Abigail called from across the yard.

"Cheryl is here! Come, come. Join our team."

A volleyball net had been set up to one side of the yard as well as a corn hole game and a place to pitch horseshoes. If Cheryl thought she would be the only guest in attendance, she had been completely wrong, but when she recognized that she was the only English person there, she realized how special her relationship with Naomi and Rebekah truly was.

She helped the women set up the makeshift tables, which consisted of wooden sawhorses with plywood sheets on the top covered in long vinyl tablecloths. Each one was clamped down with binder clips and anchored with bowls of yummy-looking food.

Cheryl grabbed a glass of lemonade then headed over to check out the volleyball game.

"Cheryl Cooper?"

She turned at the sound of her name to see Marvin Chupp walking across the road toward her. "Yes?"

"A word please?"

Cheryl hesitated for only a moment before finally giving a small nod of consent. "Sure. What's on your mind?"

"I just wanted to say that I am sorry for all the trouble I gave you while you were here."

Cheryl managed not to frown in confusion.

"I'm sure it was no matter." What else could she say?

But Marvin shook his head. "I behaved badly. And I know that now. My wife." He took off his hat and rubbed the back of his neck. "Well, she is not real happy with me. She said we should stick together and I needed to forget old bygones."

Cheryl nodded. "Well, I have no hard feelings. Maybe you should talk to Albert though."

Marvin looked stricken. "Go talk to Albert?"

"Yes, if you really want to make amends. Don't you think you should start with him?"

Marvin shook his head. "I do not think he wants to talk to me."

"You never know until you try." For a moment she thought Marvin would protest, then he gave a small nod and headed over to the grill where Albert stood flipping patties and turning hot dogs. She watched the two of them for a second, then curiosity got the better of her and she inched forward, trying to hear their conversation.

"Quit being stubborn and just apologize." This came from Marvin's wife. Cheryl just realized that the woman had followed him across the road and was standing with her hands propped upon her ample hips.

"Ja," Rebekah said. "You too, Albert. It's time this feud ended."

Each man looked at the other, neither one seemingly happy about making amends.

Marvin's wife caught Rebekah's eye. Rebekah gave a small nod then turned back to the two men. "Fine. If you do not want to apologize, that is fine. But before you go back to not speaking, one of you needs to tell me what this feud is about."

The two men turned to Rebekah, each one appearing somewhat horrified at the request.

"I do not know what it is about," Albert said. "He started it."

"I started it? I did not do anything to you. Next thing I know you're not talking to me, and I didn't do anything."

Marvin's wife looked from one of them to the other. "Are you telling me that neither one of you knows what this whole argument has been about all these years?"

"He does." Marvin and Albert both pointed to each other at the same time. Then they looked at their fingers, their gazes met, and both burst out laughing.

Rebekah and Nellie linked arms in their camaraderie as they surveyed their husbands.

"Why do you not get a plate and stay?" Rebekah asked.

Marvin and Nellie nodded. "Ja, we would like that very much."

Cheryl smiled and moved away. Wasn't that the way of it? An age-old fight and no one even remembered how it began. But thankfully this one had ended, and it looked as if good friends and wonderful companionship were all that were left on the horizon.

Once more, Cheryl thanked God for allowing her this opportunity to come to Sugarcreek. To meet these friends and have all these new experiences. She wouldn't trade them for anything in the world.

Author Letter

Dear Reader,

I can honestly say that I never thought I would be writing a book about an Amish dairy farm, and yet here it is! This book would not have been possible had it not been for the wonderful editors and staff at Guideposts, but the most invaluable input came from three young women in Lancaster, Pennsylvania.

Last September, I had the chance of a lifetime—to visit Lancaster and stay with my Amish friend while her husband took a hunting trip. Sadie's brother lives just down the road and owns a dairy farm. He graciously let me come help milk cows, not once but twice! (Secretly I think he was enjoying the free labor, but who am I to say?) Step by step, I followed behind my mentors, three of his six beautiful daughters—one sixteen, one fourteen, and one twelve.

Let me tell you, a dairy barn is noisy, big, and smelly. I had the time of my life.

All those things you hear about Amish work ethic? True. All those things about working together and helping one another? True. All those things about the Amish being standoffish and aloof? Uh, not so much. They welcomed me like one of their own, and for that I am eternally grateful. And blessed! Oh, so blessed!

When I went to Pennsylvania, this book was already in the early stages and it was the first book I finished when I returned home. That's one of the many reasons why it's so special to me.

I hope you enjoyed my tale of milk, revenge, and strange characters. It was so much fun to write. And if you know about milking, dairy barns, and cows and find a mistake, the fault is totally my own. These wonderful new friends did their best to teach me all that they know. And if nothing else, I had a great time along the way!

Blessings to you!

Amy Lillard

ABOUT THE AUTHOR

Author Amy Lillard loves nothing more than a good book. Except for her family...and maybe homemade tacos...and nail polish. But reading and writing are definitely high on the list. Born and bred in Mississippi, Amy is a transplanted Southern belle who now lives in Oklahoma with her deputy husband, their genius son, two spoiled cats, and one very lazy beagle. Oh, and don't forget the stray kitty that has taken up residence on her front porch.

When Amy isn't creating happy endings, she's chauffeuring her teen prodigy to baseball practice, guitar lessons, and orchestra concerts. She has a variety of hobbies, but her favorite is whatever gets her out of housework.

Amy is an award-winning author with more than twenty novels and novellas. She's a member of Romance Writers of America and American Christian Fiction Writers and loves to hear from readers. You can find her on Facebook, Instagram, Google+, Twitter, Goodreads, and Pinterest. For links to the various sites, visit her Web site at amywritesromance.com.

Fun Fact about
the Amish or Sugarcreek, Ohio

Not all Amish children play with faceless dolls. Believe me, I'm as disappointed as you are! But when I was in Pennsylvania, the only places with faceless dolls were the souvenir shops. That's not to say that *no* Amish children have faceless dolls. I have a doll from the very conservative community in Ethridge, Tennessee. They are Swartzentruber Amish, among the most conservative of the Old Order, and their children do play with faceless dolls. So if you're traveling around to any of the varied Amish communities in our great country, be mindful. You may be surprised by what you see!

Something Delicious from Our Sugarcreek Friends

Shoofly Pie

1 cup flour

²⁄₃ cup brown sugar

1 tablespoon vegetable oil,
   shortening, or lard

1 cup molasses

1 large egg

1 teaspoon baking soda

¾ cup boiling water

1 pie crust, either store-bought
   or your own recipe

Preheat oven to 375 degrees.

Mix together flour, brown sugar, and shortening until smooth. Set aside one-half cup of mixture.

Stir molasses, egg, and baking soda into the large portion. Add water and mix well.

Pour the filling into the unbaked pie crust. Crumble remaining sugar/flour/shortening mixture on top of the pie.

Bake for eighteen minutes at 375 degrees and then lower temperature to 350 degrees and bake for another eighteen to twenty minutes until the crust is golden and center of pie is only a bit unset. Remove and cool on a baker's rack before slicing. Serve with vanilla ice cream or whipped cream if you prefer. Enjoy!

Read on for a sneak peek of another exciting book
in the series Sugarcreek Amish Mysteries!

Earthly Treasures
by Annalisa Daughety

Every August Cheryl Cooper found herself struck by the urge to purchase school supplies. All those aisles of new crayons, pens, and blank notebooks were too tempting, despite the fact that she was several years removed from actually needing school supplies.

This year was no different.

"Do you have a little one headed back to school?" the cashier asked as she rang up a box of colored pencils.

Cheryl laughed. "No. It just seemed like a good time to stock up." She watched as the woman stuffed two boxes of crayons into a plastic bag. "And I'll donate some of this stuff to our local elementary school. I heard on the radio this morning that they'll be holding a school supply drive soon."

The woman grinned. "That's nice."

Cheryl paid and took her bags. Did she really look old enough to have kids in school? Of course she did. At thirty-one, she had many friends whose kids were either already in school or starting this year. What an odd thought though. She was old enough to be someone's mom.

Sobered by that thought, she stepped out of the cool store and into the warm sunshine. Time seemed to be passing at the speed of light now that she'd hit her thirties.

She made her way to her car, still lost in thought. A piece of bright purple paper stuck under the windshield wiper blade of her car caught her eye. She pulled the paper off and glanced at it.

"It'll be a ton of fun."

Cheryl turned to see a young woman with jet black hair holding a stack of the purple flyers.

The young woman smiled. "Caught in the act." She held up the papers. "My boss is making me do this. Putting a flyer on every car in town isn't exactly my favorite thing." She sighed. "And seriously? I have no clue what I'm supposed to do about all the buggies."

"Leave the flyer with the horse?" Cheryl asked then grinned. "Kidding."

The woman giggled. "I know, right? I called him earlier today and made that very same remark. He said just to get it done. He wants the whole town to know about our event."

"What event is that?" Cheryl asked. She opened the door on her blue Ford Focus and tossed her purchases inside then turned back to face the woman.

"A geocaching slash treasure hunt." She made a slashing motion with one hand as she said it. "I'm Laura, by the way. Laura Groves."

"Nice to meet you. I'm Cheryl Cooper." She glanced down at the flyer that was in her hand. "Geocaching?"

"You ever heard of it?"

Cheryl thought for a moment. She at least knew the concept. "Yes. Hidden treasures are all over the country. And somehow you find them." She shrugged. "Maybe I'm not very clear on how to go about it."

Laura shook her head. "You're kinda right. At least you have the general idea." She set her giant stack of flyers on the hood of Cheryl's car. "You use GPS coordinates. Normally people log on to a Web site or use the geocaching app to find them. But in this case, they aren't typical caches."

"I'm not sure I follow."

"The geocaches on the Web site are always there. People find them and log the ones they find either on the paper that is with the cache or they log it online."

"I've never understood what it is they find though."

Laura widened her smile. "Nothing big normally. And the general rule of thumb is that if you take something from the cache, you leave a treasure for the next hunter. You may find a coin and leave an eraser. Not a big prize, but it's still fun to hunt for something."

It might be the August heat, but it did sound appealing to Cheryl. "That sounds kind of fun."

"Oh, it is. Typically you sign your name and date on a little ledger that's with the hidden cache. It's fun to see all the people who've been there before you."

"So how is this going to work?" Cheryl held up the flyer.

"We've hidden some special geocaches. And there will be some other things hidden that are more like a scavenger hunt."

Cheryl skimmed over the flyer again. "Sounds interesting."

"Definitely. You should come to the big kickoff event we're hosting on Friday. I'll explain all the rules to everyone then—there's even a cash prize." Laura smiled. "All you need is a partner, and you'll be ready to join the hunt."

"Partner?" Cheryl asked.

"Yep. You'll work in teams. Believe me, you wouldn't want to try and solve some of the clues alone. They're kinda tricky." Laura tucked the stack of flyers under her arm. "I've got to run. I've got to visit a few businesses to see if I can leave stacks at their counters. But I hope to see you Friday evening. All the details are on there." She motioned toward Cheryl's flyer. "Tell your friends."

Cheryl said good-bye and climbed into her car. She was thankful the impromptu school supply run had been her last stop of the day. She'd been running errands ever since she'd placed the Closed sign on the door of the Swiss Miss. She couldn't wait to get home.

Home.

It had taken some time, but she thought of Sugarcreek as her home now. Almost exactly one year ago, her aunt Mitzi had left for Papua New Guinea to pursue a lifelong dream as a missionary. Cheryl—with a freshly broken heart and nothing important enough career-wise to keep her in Columbus—had uprooted her life and moved to Sugarcreek. She'd taken over as manager of her aunt's gift shop, the Swiss Miss, and had moved into Mitzi's adorable cottage.

Things had been shaky at first; in fact there had been times Cheryl had almost told Aunt Mitzi that the arrangement wasn't working. But soon she'd felt at home in quaint Sugarcreek, and had made some wonderful friends.

She pulled into the driveway at the cottage and collected her things. As soon as she opened the door, her cell phone rang. She dropped her bags on the couch and fished it out of her purse.

"Hi, Momma." She sank onto the couch, and her cat, Beau, jumped into her lap. "What's up?" She'd just talked to her parents the day before, a Sunday afternoon ritual they'd started when she'd first left home. "Is everything okay?"

"Is your guest room still ready for guests?" her mother asked.

Cheryl sat up. "Sure." Her parents had visited Sugarcreek a few months ago, but she'd love to see them again. "Why?"

"Do you remember your cousin Michelle? She's a bit older than you, but surely you remember her."

Cheryl thought for a moment. "Didn't she go to Ohio State? And her husband was on the football team there?"

"That's her. His name is Jared."

Michelle was about fifteen years older than Cheryl, so they hadn't been the sort of cousins who'd grown up together. "I guess I've sort of lost track of her now." Cheryl wondered if it made her an awful family member if she didn't even know for sure what state Michelle and her family lived in now. "Is she somewhere in Virginia?"

"They used to live in West Virginia years ago. But they've been near Cleveland for several years now. And she has a daughter who'll be a freshman at Ohio State this fall. Her name is Jessica. I think you may have met her when she was a baby."

"That was many moons ago, Mom."

Her mother laughed. "Yes, I suppose it was. Anyway, apparently Jessica has been wanting to visit Sugarcreek for a while. As Michelle put it, she has a slight obsession with all things Amish, and she'd love to come visit you for a few days."

"So I'd be responsible for a teenager?" Cheryl asked.

"She's going off to college in a couple weeks, so it's not like she'll need a babysitter or anything. She's following her parents' footsteps and going to Ohio State. That's why she'll be traveling through your neck of the woods in the first place." Mom sighed. "I know it's asking a lot, but do you mind if she stays with you for a few days?"

Cheryl scratched Beau behind the ears. "What will we do?" She had babysat some in high school, but those had been little kids. She wasn't exactly equipped for life with a teenager.

Mom laughed. "You just do your normal stuff. Work, spend time with your friends there. Jessica just needs a place to be her home base while she explores the area. She's an adult after all. Although...it would be nice if you took her sightseeing and maybe to one of those delicious restaurants nearby. I doubt she'll expect you or even want you to be with her 24-7."

"Okay, that sounds good."

"I'm glad, because I already told Michelle her daughter was welcome to stay."

Cheryl raked her fingers through her short red hair. She loved her mother, but sometimes the woman could drive her nuts. "Of course you did." She chuckled. "I am sure we'll have a lovely time."

"Michelle will be calling you any time now to make plans. I just wanted to give you a quick heads-up." She cleared her throat. "I think Jessica will be arriving tomorrow, but it may be Thursday instead. Michelle wasn't totally sure."

Tomorrow? Cheryl sighed. "Thanks, Momma. I love you. Tell Daddy I said hi and I love him too." They said their good-byes and hung up.

Cheryl rubbed Beau underneath his chin. "Seems like we'd better get ready for some company." So much for a quiet night at home with the book she'd checked out at the library.

She left Beau napping on the couch and went to see what kind of shape the guest room was in. It wasn't exactly pristine, but at least it wasn't too messy. She should have time to get the bedding washed while she ran to the grocery store.

Her phone dinged, signaling an incoming e-mail.

Aunt Mitzi.

The message was short and sweet.

Dearest Cheryl,

I'm having something of a crisis and need your assistance. I'll Skype you at 8 p.m. your time. Oh, Cheryl, I hope you get this and will be waiting on my call.

Much love,
Aunt Mitzi

Cheryl glanced at the clock. She had less than two hours until her aunt's call. She quickly stripped the guest bed and started the laundry as she imagined all the things that could be deemed a crisis on the mission field. Was her aunt sick? Had there been an accident? Was she in danger? Cheryl's mind raced.

Normally she wouldn't worry so much, but it wasn't like Aunt Mitzi to be so dramatic.

Cheryl said a quick prayer that everything was okay and headed out the door.

A Note from the Editors

We hope you enjoyed *Sugarcreek Amish Mysteries*, published by the Books and Inspirational Media Division of Guideposts, a nonprofit organization that touches millions of lives every day through products and services that inspire, encourage, help you grow in your faith, and celebrate God's love.

Thank you for making a difference with your purchase of this book, which helps fund our many outreach programs to military personnel, prisons, hospitals, nursing homes, and educational institutions.

We also create many useful and uplifting online resources. Visit Guideposts.org to read true stories of hope and inspiration, access OurPrayer network, sign up for free newsletters, download free e-books, join our Facebook community, and follow our stimulating blogs.

To learn about other Guideposts publications, including the best-selling devotional *Daily Guideposts*, go to Guideposts.org/Shop, call (800) 932-2145, or write to Guideposts, PO Box 5815, Harlan, Iowa 51593.

Sign up for the
Guideposts Fiction Newsletter
and stay up-to-date on the books you love!

You'll get sneak peeks of new releases, recommendations from other Guideposts readers, and special offers just for you . . .
and it's FREE!

**Just go to Guideposts.org/Newsletters
today to sign up.**

Guideposts. Visit Guideposts.org/Shop
or call (800) 932-2145

Find more inspiring fiction in these best-loved Guideposts series!

Mysteries of Martha's Vineyard

Come to the shores of this quaint and historic island and dig into a cozy mystery. When a recent widow inherits a lighthouse just off the coast of Massachusetts, she finds exciting adventures, new friends, and renewed hope.

Tearoom Mysteries

Mix one stately Victorian home, a charming lakeside town in Maine, and two adventurous cousins with a passion for tea and hospitality. Add a large scoop of intriguing mystery and sprinkle generously with faith, family, and friends, and you have the recipe for Tearoom Mysteries.

Sugarcreek Amish Mysteries

Be intrigued by the suspense and joyful "aha!" moments in these delightful stories. Each book in the series brings together two women of vastly different backgrounds and traditions, who realize there's much more to the "simple life" than meets the eye.

Mysteries of Silver Peak

Escape to the historic mining town of Silver Peak, Colorado, and discover how one woman's love of antiques helps her solve mysteries buried deep in the town's checkered past.

Patchwork Mysteries

Discover that life's little mysteries often have a common thread in a series where every novel contains an intriguing whodunit centered around a quilt located in a beautiful New England town.

To learn more about these books, visit Guideposts.org/Shop